LOVE
ON THE AIR

LOVE
ON THE AIR

•

Sierra Donovan

Text copyright ©2004 by Holly LaPat
All rights reserved.
Printed in the United States of America.

Published by Montlake Romance
P.O. Box 400818
Las Vegas, NV 89140

ISBN-13: 9781477813652
ISBN-10: 1477813659

To Charlie, for helping me find my
happily-ever-after—in this book, and in my life.

They say writing is a solitary profession. I say that was before we had computers. Thanks to modern communications, I've gotten advice and support from many writers, both published and unpublished. To name everyone would be just about impossible, but special thanks go to Carol Hutchens, Steph Newton, and the three Js—Julie Mensch, Joanna King and Jody Wallace.

To everyone who's still out there trying: It happened to me. It can happen to you too.

Chapter One

He wasn't the man she'd expected.

Dark hair. Searching brown eyes. A well-tailored black suit.

The coat of that suit was parted to accommodate a large, middle-aged midriff. The dark hair left off well above his forehead, exposing several inches of balding scalp. And his smile somehow reminded her of a frog that, when kissed, might turn into a toad.

Of course, Christie Becker wasn't sure what she'd expected from the general manager at KYOR, the radio station where she was interviewing for a job. She'd been too excited when she got the call yesterday. This afternoon, she'd pulled into the building's parking structure literally breathless. She'd forced herself to wait in her car for a few minutes while she tried to slow the pounding of her heart.

She had plenty of time. After all, she was twenty minutes early.

Now, those quizzical brown eyes scoured over her resume, as if some trace of radio experience might appear there. She had none, except for the fact that she'd finished broadcasting school three months ago. Her pulse raced and she caught herself smoothing down the hem of her dress. Again.

"Well, Miss Becker," Mr. Arboghast said, "I did have the impression you had a little more experience when Alex gave me your tape." Alex Peretti had been her teacher at broadcasting school. He was her staunch supporter, and best of all, a good friend of Ed Arboghast, the station's general manager.

"No, sir," Christie said, sitting up straight and putting out her best smile and radio voice. "Just the radio station at broadcasting school." Her smile widened. "But if you drive in a two-block circle around the building, you can pick up the signal pretty well."

It had the right effect. It made him smile. "Yes, well, maybe I'll try that some time." The smile raised the round cheeks in his full face, making his eyes almost disappear. "The point is, I listened to the tape Alex gave me. I like it." He folded his hands in the center of his nearly-empty desk blotter. Christie couldn't help thinking this man would have been out of step even when Dick Clark was rating records on American Bandstand back in the fifties. Still, he seemed to like her, and that was a good sign.

Mr. Arboghast looked at her for a moment, cocking his head to one side. Then he said, "I'm going to have you talk to our program director."

Christie felt as if she'd just been dropped into one of those dunking booths at the county fair. Her nerves, which had been lulled into a low idle, revved up again. *Talk to the program director.* That had to be good. But then why had she started off talking to the general manager, the station's official head honcho?

The "honcho" was picking up the phone, and Christie could almost hear the sound of gears being set in motion. *Oh, please, let it be true.* She'd been a liberal arts major for her first two years of college. Finally, the question people kept asking her had begun to penetrate: *What are you going to do with a liberal arts degree?* She'd always loved music, but she didn't show any special talent for performing or writing it, and the idea of teaching didn't appeal to her. A spate of business courses followed as Christie rushed to prepare herself for a career in the mythic "real world." All for what? Three mind-numbing years in a loan office.

In college, the world had been full of possibilities. She'd put her shy, mousy teenage years behind her. But as the possibilities vanished, Christie felt as if she would disappear too. She was dissolving into the background of a staid, third-floor office as her twenties ticked away.

Her dream of working in radio had kindled almost out of nowhere, but once it took hold, it caught fire. All her life, people had told her what a pretty voice she had. At last she'd decided to put that voice to some use. Something enjoyable. Something better than pushing papers eight hours a day. So she'd gone to broadcasting school in Hollywood—and, finally, found something she excelled at.

"Rick?" Mr. Arboghast was saying into the phone.

"I have someone here for you to see. An applicant for the overnight shift."

A pause. Mr. Arboghast looked at his wristwatch. "That's not for another fifteen minutes. Could you squeeze her in?"

Christie's heart sank. This man hadn't even known she was coming?

"Okay, right now. See you." He hung up and rose, scooping up the neat little folder with her resume inside. The ink blotter on his desktop was now bare.

"Let's go." He smiled at her, and she prayed she wasn't being led to the slaughter.

Following Mr. Arboghast down the corridor, Christie surreptitiously checked her appearance. She couldn't see her slip, but just to be sure, she tugged up under the waistline of the rose-patterned dress she was wearing. With its matching solid rose blazer, she'd hoped to look feminine and businesslike at the same time. When she tried it on, it had seemed like the right complement to her fair complexion and dark red hair.

More makeup? Less makeup? There was no time to check, as she was led through a very confusing series of corridors. The station was on the ground floor of an office building in Santa Moreno, a nice little town tucked away in a corner of Southern California an hour away from Los Angeles. How big could the building be, anyway?

At least she knew there was no food in her teeth. She'd checked in the rearview mirror before she got out of the car.

Mr. Arboghast stopped outside an office door, the

width of his body blocking her view into the room. Christie heard the voice coming from inside and froze.

"I've got to go, Jack," said a rich male voice. "I'm on the air in a few minutes, and something unexpected just came up." A pause. Then he laughed, a warm, deep baritone laugh that Christie felt deep down in her toes.

She knew that voice. The program director—her prospective boss—was Rick Fox. She remembered him well from the radio station she'd listened to back in college. She'd spent many a night studying in her dorm room with Rick Fox in the background. She'd admired those rich tones even then, years before she consciously thought of going into radio. Christie swallowed, resolving not to be starstruck.

"Gotta go," he said. "Talk to you next week." Mr. Arboghast stepped through the door. Christie stepped in beside him. Behind the desk was a man with light brown hair, his face turned away from them. He sat in front of a computer screen on the right-hand side of the L-shaped desk. One hand rested on the computer keyboard; the other still held the phone. Christie had the immediate impression of a man used to doing several things at once. Unlike the general manager's, his desk was heaped with stacks of papers, manila file folders and trade magazines.

Rick Fox hung up. "Hi, Ed. What have you got for me here?"

Christie wasn't sure how she felt about being referred to as a "what."

Then he swiveled around in his chair, and she drew in her breath. He was younger than she expected—

early thirties at most—and, not to put too fine a point on it, drop-dead handsome. He had thoughtful-looking gray eyes, and features that wouldn't have been out of place on a classic film actor from the forties. Christie remembered him joking on the air about having a face made for radio. He'd lied. His basic white dress shirt was open at the neck, his light brown hair slightly tousled. Careless, but not sloppy. Someone who didn't fuss too much over his appearance, which Christie found all the more attractive.

She reminded herself it was the job she was after, not the man behind the desk.

The classic features took on a startled look as his eyes fell on her. Then he stood, long legs unfolding underneath him with a smooth, masculine grace. Christie slapped herself mentally. She wasn't some teenager with a crush; she was a grown woman, interviewing for a job she desperately wanted.

"Rick," Mr. Arboghast said, oblivious to her idiocy, "this is Christie Becker. Alex Peretti sent me her tape last week, and we've just been talking." He handed the folder to Rick. Christie sensed, with a sinking feeling, that he'd never seen it before in his life. And he looked like he had a lot on his mind.

He took the package from Ed with his left hand while he reached for hers with his right. When they shook hands, Christie felt the blood go to her feet. The pressure of his fingers around hers was warm, firm and brief, but the gray eyes contemplated her for a long time. She would have given a lot to know what they saw. "Miss Becker."

"Mr. Fox." Her much-praised voice deserted her; to her own ears, she sounded about thirteen years old.

He took his seat, her folder still in hand, and motioned for her to sit in the small, straight-backed metal chair facing his desk. A lot less elaborate than Mr. Arboghast's office, Christie noted, sitting down on the hard seat. She also noted that somewhere in the last several seconds, Mr. Arboghast had disappeared.

Mr. Fox opened the little folder, wearing a preoccupied expression. She ventured, "Did I catch you at a bad time?"

He glanced up with a trace of a wry smile. "I'm afraid there's never a very good time."

This didn't bode well. "I know you're on the air in a few minutes. I could come back—"

"You're here now. It's as good a time as any."

As he leaned back and studied the contents of the folder, Christie took the opportunity to study him. He would have looked even more appealing if not for the faint frown lines appearing between his brows. Christie reminded herself once more to concentrate on the business at hand. Was he seeing anything he liked?

There wasn't much to see: her resume, a photo, and the little cassette that all her hopes were pinned on. After what seemed like three hours, but could only have been a few moments, Rick glanced up at her. "Nice eight-by-ten glossy," he said with another half-smile. It didn't sound much like a compliment.

"That was my instructor's idea," she said, hoping Alex was a friend of Rick's as well as Mr. Arboghast's. She'd wondered at the time if the picture was a good idea. After all, this wasn't a modeling job. He looked down again, and the half-smile was gone. "He thought the hair color would help me stand out," she went on. Unnerved by his silence, she added, "That really is my natural hair color."

She was prattling. Worse, she sounded like an empty-headed girl.

"Too bad," Rick Fox said dryly, his eyes still on the folder. "I was thinking of getting mine colored the same way."

She wanted to crawl into a hole and die.

Until he looked up and grinned at her.

The grin was as devastating as the wisecrack had been, for an entirely different reason. His face lost its guarded look, and all Christie could do was smile back even as she felt her face flush. Maybe things would get better from here.

They didn't. Returning to her resume, he got to the subject she couldn't escape. "I see you're working now as a loan processor."

"That's right." Only two syllables, but at least it wasn't stupid. And she didn't squeak.

"I'm a little puzzled, Miss Becker. You've got three years of solid experience at that job. You're making a lot more there than you would starting out as a disc jockey here. Why would you want to leave?"

"Ever work in a loan office?"

"No." The smile was back. It brought out pleasant crinkles around his eyes. "Pretty exciting?"

"Death defying. If you want to die of boredom." She pulled in a breath, remembering to bring her voice up from her diaphragm the way she'd been taught. "That's just it. I've spent three years in an office making decent money, but it's nothing I really care about. That's why I went to broadcasting night school. I want something I can put my heart into." No need to go into the rest. How one day she'd looked down at the cheap veneer of her desk and almost sworn she could see herself fading into it.

"Well, Miss Becker, radio isn't all it's cracked up to be either. It's not nearly as glamorous as you might think. Disc jockeys eat a lot of Top Ramen, especially when they're first starting out. And I'm afraid advancement isn't exactly guaranteed either. Vacant air shifts don't come up very often here, except for the overnight shift. Did Ed tell you what the job pays?"

"No, we didn't get to that."

He told her. She tried not to wince. She said, "I've got some money put away."

"And you realize the shift is from midnight to 6 A.M." He studied her again, faint frown lines creasing his brow once more.

"Yes, I'm fine with that." Would he please ask about her qualifications? Christie needed to get on comfortable ground. *Speak up. Elaborate*, she told herself. She opened her mouth—to say what, she didn't know. Things had gone so well with the general manager, she'd been caught off guard. *One more minute and you're out the door. You don't know when you'll get another shot. You've got to make this one count.* "Have you heard my tape?" There. That was something.

"No." Rick passed a hand roughly through his hair. It added to that attractively tousled look. *Stop it*, she thought. *This man is about to squash your livelihood.*

"To be honest, Miss Becker," he was saying, "I wasn't expecting you when you came in. And—"

"Well, do me a favor." Something rose up within her, and she hoped it wasn't a bad thing. "Before you make up your mind, please listen to my tape." She was encouraged to hear her voice come out confident, instead of plaintive, the way she felt. "I know I haven't had a full-time air shift yet, but I did complete broadcasting school, and Alex Peretti thought enough of me to recommend me." She prayed, once again, that Alex's name held some clout with him. "Listen to the tape, and if you like what you hear, give me a chance to show you what I can do. I promise you won't be disappointed."

She had his attention. At least he was looking at her, although she couldn't read his expression.

"The 'B' side of the tape has some commercial demos," she went on. "Of course, they're only dummy spots I did at school. But I think you'll agree production is one of my strong points. I imagine that comes in handy, especially on the overnight shift." She smiled. "I've heard what radio deadlines are like." She felt better. Much, much better. Oxygen was starting to return to her lungs. And her brain.

Rick promptly deflated her. "Well, Miss Becker, that's true. But we do our best to take care of that during the day, when we can play the spots for client approval."

"I'm very good with sound levels," she came back quickly, but with less confidence.

"Yes. Well." He glanced down at her package again, no longer handling any of the materials, and

Christie had the feeling she'd already been discarded. "I'll give your tape a listen. But I can't make any promises. I'm sure you were a good student, or Peretti wouldn't have sent you here. But there's really no substitute for on-air experience."

He stood, and she knew the interview was over. She forced herself to stand and held out her hand one more time. When he took it, she made sure to make eye contact again. And tried not to sink into those contemplative gray eyes. "Thanks for your time, Mr. Fox."

"I'll give you a call," he said, and something in his voice was a little softer. It sounded like the end of a bad blind date.

Mr. Arboghast was nowhere to be seen as Rick showed her back down the twisting corridors. She was sure she was seeing the inside of the station, and Rick Fox, for the last time. Annoyingly, the thought gave her two pangs instead of just one. He hadn't even been particularly nice to her.

The glass doors eased shut behind her. At least it didn't hit her on the way out. A girl, that's what he'd seen her as. A kid. She headed toward the parking garage without looking back.

I shouldn't have worn pink, she thought.

Rick watched the rose-clad figure walk away with her head held high, looking taller than she actually was. The straight posture probably carried quite a bit of injured pride along with it. But it couldn't be helped. A loan processor with no on-air experience? What was Ed thinking of, anyway? Still, a part of him was sorry to see her go. No redhead had the right to look that good in pink.

But that wasn't the point.

Rick got into the on-air studio two minutes before 4:00 P.M. when his afternoon drive shift started. Jonathan, the disc jockey on the air before him, had stacked up all the CDs and commercials for the first hour. It left Rick with little to think about until five o'clock, when he'd start airing the news and traffic reports. Then things would get hectic.

After the first song, he opened the microphone. "KYOR—*your* station for the best songs of yesterday and today," he said. "This is Rick Fox, taking you through your afternoon drive." He had a vision of a certain redhead hearing him on her car radio, ripping the knob off the dash and throwing it out the window.

Guilt, he told himself. That was all it was.

Whatever it was, it sent him into his office, down the hall from the studio, the first time he played a song more than five minutes long. That would give him enough time to listen to her tape. Enough of her tape, at least, to confirm his opinion and ease his conscience. Keeping an eye on the clock above the door of his office, he found the cassette and popped it into the boom box on his desk.

Christie's voice came out at him—full, bright and just a little stiff. *Not bad for a beginner, actually. Not bad at all.*

The first side of the cassette was the air check—excerpts of Christie's announcer breaks from an on-air shift, with the songs edited out. It used up most of his five minutes, but Rick listened all the way through it, telling himself he was nuts. He looked at the chair across from his desk, where she'd sat less than half an hour ago. The memory was so fresh that he could still see her there, quiet determination in her green-hazel eyes, legs crossed distractingly under the soft pastel skirt.

Shaking himself, he got up, went down the hall and started the next song. A moment later he was back to flip the tape over and listen to those commercial demos Christie Becker was so proud of.

She had a right to be. Unless someone else was pushing all the buttons for her, and Rick somehow doubted it, she had a wonderful feel for production. She even worked in a few sound effects, without going overboard, a common pitfall for beginners. And the way she read the scripts was something no one could fake for her. She sounded natural, confident and vibrant, far more seasoned than her brief training should have allowed. Her voice was in the soprano range, but not too high. It would make a nice contrast to the lower, huskier voice of his midday disc jockey, Yvonne. Their commercials could go back-to-back without sounding anything alike.

He'd told Christie a half-truth. They did try to get commercials recorded during business hours, for client approval, but "try" was the operative word. A lot of production did get done after hours for approval the next day, often after the spots had already started airing.

When Christie's commercial demos ended, the sound of blank tape hiss filled the room. *Well?* it seemed to prod him.

Sitting back in his chair, Rick picked up the glossy color photo he'd teased her about. The young woman in the picture looked back at him, her chin resting on her hands, eyes sparkling with a pixie's smile. *Trouble*, his mind flashed. What was it about her? He'd worked around pretty women before, and he'd always had enough sense to keep it professional. He'd never gone out with any coworker, let alone one who worked under him. At this station, it wasn't just a bad idea. It was an ironclad company policy: no dating between supervisors and employees.

Since his divorce, it had become a reflex for him to keep his feelings in check, both in and out of the office. So why worry about Christie?

No reason, he decided. It just bothered him to see someone like her, with a decent career already under way, charging headlong into a business that had cost him so much. A business that had cost him his marriage. A business he'd tried to walk away from once, and failed. Because once it got into your blood, that was it.

Do you know what you're getting into? he asked her silently.

Her smile sparkled back at him, unfazed. Rick was sure he would have gotten much the same reaction if he'd asked her the question in person.

And then he remembered he had a song about to fade, if it hadn't already. He bolted for the studio. Dead air, as he told all his employees, was the eighth deadly sin.

He made it back just before the music ran out.

*   *   *

An old movie. A cup of hot tea. A bowl of popcorn and M&Ms. Comfort foods.

Christie lined them all up as she settled into her apartment that night to lick her wounds. She curled up on the couch under the pink and gray afghan her aunt had crocheted for her when she was in high school. Tomorrow was another day at the loan office, another day of being professional and civilized, surrounded by men in suits fifteen years older than she was. The suits, probably, as well as the men. Tonight she'd be a kid again, and shut out the mental replay of the disastrous interview—all the things she'd said wrong, all the things she hadn't said but should have. She was a kid who wanted her mother, but she hadn't called her yet. Talking about it right now would just be another way of reliving her failure.

Alex Peretti had been nice enough to recommend her and she'd blown it. Her one chance to work at the only radio station within a workable driving distance. Now it was time to search for a job on her own, the way she should have in the first place. Start sending out tapes to stations in other areas. Not Los Angeles; she didn't kid herself that she was ready for a market that size. Which meant, if she was going to find a radio job, she'd have to face the prospect of relocating. She'd known that when she enrolled in broadcasting school. Expecting to end up at the one station right in her own back yard—well, she'd been dreaming.

If it weren't for the stupid hill between the station's transmitter and Orangewood, where she lived and worked, at least she would have known Rick Fox was there. Then she would have been prepared for the possibility of meeting the voice from her college days. But even that wouldn't have prepared her for the way he looked. If he'd been just as unreceptive, but twenty years older, would she have been so rattled?

She picked up the remote control and started the movie. The point of this night was to forget all that for a while. She'd start on plan "B" tomorrow, a little older and wiser.

Bette Davis had barely killed her sister when the phone rang.

Christie sighed. She'd forgotten to bring the cordless phone in with her. She paused the movie and padded to the kitchen in her worn fleece slippers.

"Hello?"

"May I speak to Christie Becker, please." No telemarketer sounded like that. The voice on the other end was bigger than life. Christie recognized it immediately, but she couldn't believe it.

Deep breath. Bring your voice up from your diaphragm. "This is she," she said, putting a note of question into her voice. As if she didn't know which big-voiced male might be calling her apartment at— she glanced at the clock above the stove—seven-thirty at night? Of course. He would have just gotten off the air.

"This is Rick Fox from KYOR. We were short on time this afternoon, and I'd like to go over a few more things with you. Can you come back in?"

Chapter Two

And so it was that the next day, Christie found herself back where she'd never expected to be again: sitting across the desk from Rick Fox.

She'd traded in yesterday's rose dress for a navy blazer and slacks, hoping to erase any impression of a ditzy girl. Maybe it helped, because this time, as she sat down, he offered her coffee.

"No, thanks. Coffee makes me bounce off the walls."

"Okay. But if you take this shift, you may find yourself wanting to bounce off the walls by six in the morning."

A joke, and a reference to possible employment, right off the bat? Must not be the same man.

Rick sipped his own coffee from an impressive-sized black mug with a huge handle. As he looked across the desk at her, his eyes were quietly assessing, but definitely more approachable than yesterday.

17

Christie shifted her gaze back to the giant coffee cup, determined this time not to be distracted by a simple case of good looks. Focusing on the cup, she noticed two things: Rick Fox was left-handed, and he didn't wear a wedding ring.

"You're here on your lunch break?" he asked. Christie nodded. "Okay. I'll try to keep it short. I wanted to go over a few things with you again, so if I repeat myself, please bear with me."

He sat back, coffee cup in hand. It was a much more relaxed posture than she'd seen yesterday, although it did put him at more of a distance. He'd cleaned the top of his desk, or at least condensed it into one large stack of papers in the far right-hand corner. A lone manila folder sat at the center of the desktop in front of him. She assumed her resume was inside, but he didn't glance at it.

"Your tape surprised me," he said. "Your reads are excellent. And whoever helped you out on the effects did you proud."

"No one helped me," she said, trying not to sound indignant.

"I didn't think so." He surprised her with a grin. "Sorry. Trick question." He sipped his coffee. "First off, I want you to think again about the hours. I mean, *really* think about it. You'd be driving to work in the dark; part of the year it would still be dark by the time you went home. In between, you've got six hours alone in the building. It's a strange schedule."

"I have thought about it. I wouldn't want to do it for a million years, but to be honest, I don't plan on doing overnights for a million years." *Too outspoken?*

He didn't show any reaction either way. "How do you feel about the drive? Remember, it's two trips a night, and you have to drive it with your eyes open both ways. Do you live far from the station?"

"About fifteen minutes," she hedged. It was more like twenty-five.

"Do you have a boyfriend?"

"Excuse me?" She felt her cheeks warm. He was way out of bounds with that one.

As if he'd read her mind, Rick held up a hand. "Don't sic the labor relations board on me just yet. What I mean is, the hours of this job can put a real strain on personal relationships. The questions I'm asking you right now, I want you to ask yourself. You don't have to answer out loud if you don't want to. Do you have a boyfriend, husband, fiancé? High-maintenance cat? Anyone who'd be affected by your hours?"

"No." It wasn't any big secret, she reasoned. And, dicey questions or not, she wanted this job.

"This gig also cuts down your chances of starting up a new relationship, at least for those first million years when you're doing overnights. Any problem with that?"

"No."

He studied her for a long time, and a silence stretched out. Christie found that having Rick's full attention was no less nerve-racking than his preoccupied attitude the day before. He could look very serious when he wasn't smiling, and very intent. She wanted to shift her eyes to his coffee cup again, but didn't dare. It seemed important not to look away. Instead, she lowered her glance toward his full, firm mouth, and found that didn't help at all.

Just when the moment began to feel like a long freeze-frame, he took one more sip from his mug. "Last question," he said.

Already?

"It's a biggy." Rick sat forward, setting his coffee aside and resting his arms on his desk. "Here's where I turn into the bad guy. But I have to. I've got to take one last shot at being the voice of reason here."

Uh-oh.

"Miss Becker, you're about twenty-three years old—"

"You're not supposed to ask me that. It's illegal."

"I'm not asking you. I'm telling you."

"Twenty-six."

A smile flickered in his eyes. "Okay, you're roughly twenty-six years old, and—I can't stress this enough—you *have* a viable career. In a stable business. Broadcasting is not stable. We happen to be a privately-owned station with a pretty low turnover, but that's not the norm. Radio stations are bought and sold. Music formats change. All of which can put you out of a job. And since, as you mentioned, you're interested in advancement, there's a good chance it won't be here. Remember—low turnover. So eventually you'd probably want to move on, which means relocating, which means more instability." He paused. "And the hours—nights, personal appearances on weekends—can turn your personal life upside down. Are you prepared—"

"You said that last one already."

"Right." He smiled ruefully. "I'm not getting through to you, am I?"

It was the strangest interview she'd ever had, but it was still better than the one yesterday. Today, at least, he was really talking to her. Maybe that was what gave her the nerve to ask, "I don't mean to be rude, but do you always try to talk your applicants out of the job?"

"No. Most of them already know better. It's just too late." He shook his head. "You see, Miss Becker, besides everything else I just mentioned, radio's an addictive job. If you don't crack in three months, you may not *want* to go back to anything else. It's kind of like the priesthood: if you can be happy doing anything else, you probably should."

"What about you?"

He paused a moment before he answered. "One divorce," he said quietly. "Other than that, it's been a piece of cake."

Oops. She hadn't been going for anything that personal. "I'm sorry."

"Not your fault."

"You're still here," she noted.

"Still here. But I'm an addict, remember?" If he was any the worse for wear, Christie could see it only in the faint lines around his eyes when he smiled. All the lines really did was make him look a bit more complex than a man in his twenties. And much more interesting. She bit her lower lip.

"Would you do it again?" she asked. "Radio, I mean. Not the divorce."

"Hold on. I'm supposed to be asking the questions."

"You asked me to think about it. I'm just trying to make an informed decision."

He grinned. "Okay." He shifted his glance just beyond her, drumming the fingers of his bare left hand on the desktop as his smile faded. "Would I do it again?"

Christie suspected she'd stumbled onto something. She'd asked the handsome program director a question he'd never asked himself. Whether that was good or bad, she'd soon find out.

She didn't have long to wait. When Rick's eyes returned to hers, they were decisive. "Yes," he said. "I'd do it again."

In return for that honest answer, she tried for a few seconds to consider everything he'd warned her about. She couldn't. She wanted the job too badly. She went out on one more limb. "Well," she said, "how about if we make a bet on whether or not I crack in three months?"

Rick didn't miss a beat. "That just happens to be your probationary period." He picked up the manila file folder in front of him and flipped it across the desk in front of her. "You'll need to fill these forms out for our personnel office before you start. And forget it. I'm not betting against you."

Rick walked Christie through the station to give her a brief tour before she went back to give her two weeks' notice at the loan office.

He'd tried, he thought. No one could say he hadn't tried. But he'd already known that trying to reason with Christie was a losing battle. He knew that single-minded, feverish look, because he'd worn it himself over ten years ago when he'd quit college for his first full-time radio gig. If her work ethic matched her obvious passion, he'd made a sound business decision.

But in the hall, Rick found himself fighting the urge to guide her by touching her arm or her shoulder. To anyone else, the gesture might not have looked out of place, but he knew himself better. Her delicate build invited him to touch, and it was bringing out a lot of useless impulses—some of them protective, some of them not.

Oh, well. She was working nights. He'd hardly ever see her.

When he showed her the production room where the commercials were recorded, Christie was like a kid on Christmas morning. Most disc jockeys had to be shoved in that direction, but she was admiring everything from the computer recording console to the voice processor. Rick stayed back, leaning against the door jamb as he watched her move from one discovery to the next. "Better than the toys at broadcasting school?" he said.

"I'll say." Christie was studying the CDs of background music and sound effects, mounted on their large wall rack. She fingered the spines of the CDs with a look that bordered on avarice. *Dreaming of commercials to come?* Unusual, especially in a female jock. But as she stood there, that soft-looking auburn page boy framing her face, there was no denying how female she was.

If she could get that worked up over a CD library, maybe she did belong here. But Rick had something better in store for her than production discs. Already anticipating her reaction, he cleared his throat.

She looked up, startled, and he held back a smile. "You'd probably like a look at the on-air studio?"

The light in her eyes was even brighter than he'd expected.

Christie wasn't sure her feet were touching the ground as she walked down the hall to the last door on the left. The studio. Her holy grail. Rick opened the door and stood back for her to go in ahead of him; he was polite about things like that, she noticed. Christie scrupulously checked the "ON AIR" light above the doorway, but of course it was off. She stepped inside and nearly walked into the black Formica countertop that took up most of the room, surrounding the disc jockey on three sides.

The woman on the other side of the counter was about thirty, Hispanic-looking and very pretty, with long, chocolate brown hair that stopped one shade shy of black. As Christie and Rick entered, she smiled, pulling off her headphones. "Hi, Rick. What's up?"

"Yvonne, this is Christie Becker, our new overnight jock. Christie, this is Yvonne Reyes, our midday personality."

"A girl!" Yvonne's smile widened, and she offered her hand over the large console that stood on the counter between them. Christie scanned the enthusiasm for cattiness and found none. "About time, Rick," Yvonne said. "Now I won't have to be on every one of the nail salon spots."

"Hi." Christie shook Yvonne's hand and peered

over the console, trying to get a better look at the sliding controls on the other side. *Soon enough*, she told herself.

"Yvonne's also our music director, and my right arm. Yvonne, I'll need you to train Christie for a couple of days before her first air shift."

"Great. She can learn from my mistakes. Nice to meet you, hon."

"Yvonne Reyes," Christie said when they were outside again. "That's a pretty name." She caught herself watching Rick for his response, wondering just how attached to his right arm he might be. The woman was certainly an eyeful.

No reaction that Christie could see. "Her last name's really Reynaldo. She just tweaked it a little bit. Come to think of it, we need an air name for you, don't we?"

"Christie Becker is it," she said. "It's my mother's maiden name."

"You applied for work under an assumed name? Good thing I didn't call your references." He blinked; obviously he hadn't meant to say that. "But I will now," he amended.

"It's okay. Everybody knows about the radio thing, even at the loan office. I couldn't go to broadcasting school for a year and a half and keep my mouth shut."

"Christie Becker." He said her name slowly, as though he were tasting it. "Works for me." Christie found herself watching his lips, and reminded herself to cut it out. "What's your real last name?" he asked.

"Swensen."

"Becker, Swensen. . .German and Swedish?" She nodded. "So where'd the red hair come from?"

"The mailman was Scottish."

He threw his head back and laughed—that wonderful, rich laugh she'd heard from out in the hallway yesterday. And once again, something inside her responded to the sound. At times he seemed so cool and reserved, but not when he laughed.

"So, what's *your* real name?" she asked.

"Foxborough." It sounded Scottish. It seemed best not to mention that.

"Good," she said instead. "I was having a hard time calling you Mr. Fox. It sounds like something out of Peter Rabbit."

He chuckled again. "So that's why no one here calls me 'Mister.' " He shook his head, still smiling. "It's Rick. First names around here."

He was leading her back out the way she'd come in. By now the maze of hallways was starting to make sense. The layout was basically a horseshoe, with the programming offices on one side, including Rick's office, the production room, and the on-air studio. In the center was a small break room, and now they were passing by the sales and administrative offices on the side where she'd first come in. Rick pointed them out, but didn't spend a great deal of time talking about them. It was obvious his main concern was at the other end of the building.

At the front entrance, Rick stopped. "One more thing. Before I forget." He rested a hand over the frame of the glass door, and his blue shirt stretched taut over a lean, firm-looking waist. She had to stop noticing things like that. Rick's words pulled her back. "I had one other reservation about hiring you, and I should have mentioned it before. I've never had a woman working nights, and I'm not crazy about it, for security reasons. I want you to be careful. You probably noticed the outside wall of the studio is one big window. Keep the blinds closed. When you're walking to your car, have your keys ready, and make sure you park under a light. We've never had any problems, but I don't want you to be the first."

The serious look had returned to his gray eyes. He was about six-two, nearly a foot taller than Christie, and for a moment she felt absurdly sheltered as he stood over her. She could almost kid herself that his protective attitude was more than gentlemanly concern.

It didn't matter. He was her boss, not her boyfriend, and she could take care of herself. She decided to let him know that. "And if someone does come after me," she said, "I go for the eyes and groin."

He stared at her for half a second. "Remind me not to mess with you." He swung the door open, and once again he was all business. "Bring the forms back to personnel when you get a chance, and I'll see you in two weeks."

This time, once again, Christie made sure not to look back as she walked out. Last time it had been to preserve her dignity. This time, she was fighting the urge to see if two gray eyes were looking after her.

She'd dated very little since she'd started work at the loan office. Her job didn't put her in contact with many men, except the ones who were half of a married couple trying to finance a house. She'd gone out with one fellow student from broadcasting school, but he'd been so vain and shallow he'd bored her to tears. Maybe that explained her reaction to Rick Fox. Boring he wasn't. Conservative, maybe, but interesting, especially that streak of humor.

It didn't matter. Christie wasn't about to be side-tracked. With her goal at hand, her new boss was the last man in the world she was going to get involved with.

Chapter Three

"So keep it here on KYOR—*your* station for the best songs of yesterday and today." Yvonne turned and nodded to Christie, who was already hitting the button to shut off the microphone. The music, which had been automatically muted when the microphone was on, came back on in the studio.

It was Christie's second day of training. Yesterday, she had watched. Today, when Christie walked in, Yvonne had announced the board was hers. Yvonne still did the talking on the air, but Christie was in charge of all the buttons and sliders—starting the songs, controlling the volume, turning the microphone on and off.

Yvonne gave her a thumbs-up. "You're doing great." She picked up her cup of noodles, which had been steaming under its paper lid for the last several minutes. Apparently Rick hadn't been kidding about Top Ramen.

"So, do you lose weight eating that stuff?"

Yvonne shook her head. "No, because it makes you so thirsty you drink twice as much soda." She hoisted a can of cola toward Christie to attest.

The real studio at KYOR was much more daunting than the broadcasting school's miniature version, with about three times the number of controls to worry about. Then there was the EAS binder, the notebook to turn to in case of a signal from the Emergency Alert System. Christie lived in fear of a fire or flood her first night on the air, but Yvonne assured her she'd never known anyone who'd received a real emergency alert. The important thing was a passing familiarity with the book, in case of a surprise inspection by the FCC.

Somehow, that wasn't very reassuring.

A few minutes later, Christie fired the next song, and they were assaulted by a barrage of hard rock chords. For the first time, Yvonne took over, hastily reaching past Christie to advance the CD player a few tracks ahead. A softer track came on, and KYOR's light adult contemporary sound was restored.

"Sorry." Yvonne patted her shoulder. "I had to get that off in a hurry. We don't want people in offices diving under their desks." She pointed to the CD player. "Remember to double-check which song you have cued up after you load in the disc. These are compilation CDs. Most of the songs fit our format, but every once in a while you'll get an ancient oldie, or something that can peel paint, like that one."

"I'm sorry," Christie said. "I just hope you have an audience left after today."

"Oh, shut up." Yvonne waved her off. "That's what

today is all about—getting some of the kinks out." She sipped her soda. "Nervous about tonight?"

Christie nodded. "I've wanted this for so long, and I'm afraid if I don't do it right—" She cringed, still hearing those heavy metal chords in her head.

"Then there's tomorrow night. This isn't do or die, sweetie. I'll tell you right now, you're *going* to make mistakes." She scooped another bite of noodles from the styrofoam cup. "The great thing about radio," she said, "is it's always going forward. No one remembers if you screwed up your last break."

"Sounds like another Rick-ism."

Yvonne nodded. "And what's the worst thing a jock can do?"

They said it together: "Dead air." And laughed.

Christie had heard a lot of the Gospel According to Rick these past two days, but she'd seen very little of the man himself. He was still a mystery. When she did see him, he seemed to have reverted back to the man she'd met on her first interview—polite, but pre-occupied. Both mornings, he'd poked his head into the studio for a brief greeting that included both Yvonne and herself. Other than that, he spent most of the time in his office, and while the door was always open, Christie wasn't going to venture into that inner sanctum without a clear-cut invitation. There seemed to be at least two Rick Foxes: the cool, remote one she'd interviewed with the first time, and the one whose legs had nearly buckled laughing at her joke in the hallway. Christie didn't want to worry about which one she was going to get, and as long as she did her job well, she told herself it didn't matter.

"So," Christie said, "if you do get dead air, what happens?"

"Are you kidding?" Yvonne looked horrified. "He'll kill you."

"Really?"

Yvonne laughed. "Yes, *really*. Haven't you noticed all the severed heads hanging out there in the hall-way?" She squeezed Christie's arm. "Sorry. But you've got to lighten up, honey. You'll do fine."

Christie went in an hour before her air shift and recorded the commercials that had been assigned to her. Then she headed into the studio, trying to feel as if she did it every night of her life.

The disc jockey getting off the air was dark-haired, good-looking, and clearly aware of it. "Hi." He started the next song. "I'm Rob Gibbons."

"I'm Christie Becker," she said, trying to take some strength from the sound of her air name.

Rob turned away to pull a few CDs from the shelf above the counter, adding them to a stack he'd already started. Resting a hand on the discs, he turned back to her. "There's your first hour."

"Thanks."

"Don't thank me. Part of the job. Just make sure you do the same for McKeon before he comes in, or he'll chew you up." Christie hadn't heard much about Mark McKeon, the morning show host, but Yvonne had warned her not to step on his toes.

Rob aimed a smile at her. "Rick's hiring them cuter," he said, watching unabashedly for her reaction.

She decided to play it light, matching the tone in which it was offered. "Thank you, *Mr.* Gibbons."

Rob shrugged good-naturedly and slipped into a bulky black jacket. Clearly, he wasn't interested in sticking around to hold her hand when she started. Just as well. She wasn't sure just what else a hand-holding from Rob might entail. He stepped around to the outside of the counter. "It's all yours."

She'd waited nearly two years for this, and now she was scared to death. It must have shown. Rob stopped on his way out the door. "This your first radio gig?"

She nodded.

"Two words," he told her.

"Top Ramen?"

"How'd you know?"

He closed the door behind him, and she was alone in the studio.

Christie stepped behind the counter. It felt different, bigger than it had these past two days when she'd sat next to Yvonne. Christie started the next song on schedule, and watched the time count backward on the CD player's digital display. When it was over, it would be time for her to talk.

With a minute to go, she put her headphones on. She was so nervous she could feel the black foam cushions shaking on her ears.

The song was fading. Show time.

Christie took a deep breath and turned on the microphone. "KYOR—*your* station for the best songs of yesterday and today," she said, relieved when the voice in her headphones came back at her warm and full, instead of small and scared. "This is Christie

Becker, with you 'til 6 A.M.," she went on, pushing
the button for the next song. It started up behind her,
slow and sultry. The music steadied her, reminding her
what she was here for. She rode the volume level as
she continued. "So whatever you're up doing tonight,
I'll do it with you." A few seconds left of the song
intro. She timed it out with the beat of the song. "It's
five past midnight. Here's Sheryl Crow." Up with the
music, off with the microphone.

So far, so good. She pulled her headphones down
around her neck with a huge sigh of relief.

Now, *that's* a first break, Rick thought.

He'd told himself he wasn't going to listen. A jock's
first shift at any new station was bound to be rough.
Better to tune in a few nights later, after she'd gotten
her sea legs. But he hadn't been able to resist. It was
her first shift anywhere, except the broadcasting school
station, which really didn't count. He had to see how
it went.

And he had to admit, Christie sounded just fine. The
first break between songs was smooth; he noticed
again that she had nice timing. But he'd known that
from her tape. He didn't have to stay up past midnight
to find that out.

Not that he was in the habit of getting to bed early.
His air shift didn't end until 7 P.M. and he was rarely
out of the station before eight. Often it was a lot later.
Which led to late dinners, and then the often lengthy
process of unwinding. Most nights, three things in his
apartment's crowded living room competed for his attention: the piano at one end, the exercise treadmill at

the other, and the television set smack in the center. The treadmill ran a distant third.

Christie did her next break when she was supposed to, not succumbing to a new jock's temptation to open the microphone at every opportunity, not trying to be the next generation's answer to Rick Dees. She stuck to the basics, but her basics were solid. Christie didn't sound nearly as green as her resume, or even her tape, had led him to expect.

"Santa Moreno's best mix," she purred a moment later. Her voice had a nice quality, not husky, but with a certain sexy texture to it. The male audience would like her. Whatever kids, drunks and truckers were listening at this hour. Or divorced program directors. Rick left the stereo on as he headed down the hall to get ready for bed.

He was brushing his teeth when it happened. The song stuck, and Rick heard the familiar thrumming noise of a CD stuck in the player. He started counting the seconds until she recovered; it was an automatic reflex. *One*-one-thousand, *two*-one-thousand. . .

Come on, he thought, *you can do it.*

. . .*five*-one thousand, *six.* . .

Christie grabbed the next CD from the top of the stack and slid it into the player labeled CD-3. A moment later, she was rewarded with the chords of an old Bryan Adams song. Not the next song on the printed music log, but way better than that thrumming noise. Quickly, she pulled the volume down on the stalled CD player. *I should have done that before.*

She tried to pull the failed disc out of CD-2. It wouldn't come out. *Uh-oh. Tell me I didn't break it.*

The phone rang, one more note for the symphony of her jangled nerves. She went to pick it up, then thought, *wait.* She cued the next song in CD-1, careful to set it for the right track, so she'd be ready for the next break. Then she answered the phone.

"KYOR," she said in her best professional radio voice. Belatedly she noticed the call had come in on the hotline, the one reserved for on-air business.

"Is it CD-2 again?" She recognized Rick's voice, not that he bothered to identify himself. *Well, hello to you too.*

"Yes."

"It does that," he said. "We just got it back from the repair shop last week. Either they didn't do the job right, or it's really on its last legs. Use a butter knife."

"What?"

"A butter knife. Slip in a butter knife from the kitchen and you can get the disc out. I wouldn't bother trying to use the player again tonight, though."

"Thanks." She looked at the display, counting the time backward on the song, trying to calculate whether she had time for a run down the hall to the kitchen before her next song. *3:06 to go.*

"Oh, and Christie?" She heard a little edge of humor creep into the deep voice.

"What?" *How am I doing?*

"That song isn't on the play list."

Rats. She started to grope for another disc.

"Go ahead and leave it on. It's not out of format."

"Okay," she said. *2:37 to go.*

"And Christie?"

She shut her eyes tight and braced herself. "What?"

"You sound good."

A ton of bricks fell off her shoulders. "Thanks." It was the first nice thing she could remember him saying to her since the day she was hired, and she was annoyed at how gratifying it felt. "I'd better get that butter knife."

"You do that. Have a good night."

She hung up, refusing to ponder the nuance of his words like a lovesick sophomore. She sprinted to the kitchen, opened a few drawers and found a butter knife sharing a drawer with a million plastic forks, a few stray napkins, and a slew of fast-food salsa packets.

She returned to the studio just before her song faded. As she cued the other CD player and tried to free the jammed disc, she glanced above the shelf to see a butter knife that had clearly been left there for just that purpose.

"Way to tell me about the butter knife," she said to Yvonne the next afternoon.

Yvonne spun around on the studio's tall stool. "Oh, hon, I'm sorry. I didn't think. We just got the thing back from the shop. I thought it was okay." She made a face. "If it's any consolation, it did the same thing to me this morning."

"Mark didn't tell you? I warned him."

Yvonne shrugged. "That's McKeon for you." Mark McKeon had been every bit as pleasant as Rob had led her to expect, with barely two words of greeting for her and no introduction. "So, other than that, how'd it go?"

"I made it through. I don't think I did any permanent damage, at least."

"I'm sure you were fine. So what brings you back here so soon, anyway? You're about ten hours early for your next shift."

"Well, really, I wondered if there was anything I could do for you. I'm not used to having so many hours free during the day, and—" Christie broke off. "Oh, heck, who am I kidding? I just couldn't stay away. I'll help you with anything I can get my hands on. As long as I'm not getting in your way."

"Beginner's fever?" Something glinted in Yvonne's eyes, and Christie could see her considering the possibilities. Then the hot line rang. "Hang on. Rick's out on a live broadcast." She flipped the switch that let her use the microphone to talk over the phone line. "Hey, babe. How's it going out there?" Hearing the casual familiarity gave Christie a prickly little feeling that she didn't like.

"Running out of prizes." Rick's voice boomed cheerily out of the monitor speakers overhead. "And we've got an hour to go. I was thinking about holding a drawing for the station van. Or Ed's Mercedes. What do you think?"

Yvonne chuckled. "It's your funeral." She started the machine to record the break. "Ready when you are."

Rick's voice shifted into full-on announcer mode. "Hi, Yvonne, I'm here at the grand opening of Mich-

elle's Crafts and Collectibles, here on Fifth and Han-
cock, where they've got . . ."

Rick went on with his professional spiel, and Christie tried to examine that prickly feeling. Or smother it.
Why should she care if Yvonne flirted with Rick, or
whether there was anything behind it? That kind of
jealousy was kid stuff, and she'd outgrown it a long
time ago. There was no call for it now. Anyway,
Christie reminded herself, Yvonne was always calling
her "hon." And wouldn't she be a little more discreet
if there was really something going on?

". . . We'll be out here 'til three, so stop on by. This
is Rick Fox with KYOR, your station for the best
songs of yesterday and today."

Yvonne stopped the recording. "Thanks, handsome."

"You got it, gorgeous." Christie prickled again.
"Wish me luck out here."

"Luck out there." Unexpectedly, Yvonne turned the
microphone in Christie's direction. "Hey, say hi to
Christie."

"Christie?" His tone changed abruptly. "What's she
doing there?"

Yvonne looked startled. She grimaced at Christie,
who quietly pushed the microphone back toward
Yvonne. "She just dropped by, wanted to see if she
could help out. I thought I'd show her some stuff when
I get off the air. Maybe straighten up that mess we
call a production room."

"Okay—just make sure you get your own work
done."

Yvonne blinked at the monitor speakers. "Not a

problem. Talk to you later." She cut off the phone with a frown.

Christie said, "Is he always like that?"

Yvonne shook her head, still frowning at the speakers. "No. Never." She set the machine to play back Rick's recorded break after the next song. "He must be having a bad day."

"It didn't sound like it, until my name came up. Do you think I got on his bad side somehow?"

"In three days? Don't be silly. Anyway, you've hardly been around him."

"He's always like that with me. I mean, he goes back and forth. Like when he called last night—"

"Rick was listening at midnight? On your first shift?"

"Is that unusual?"

"Nah," Yvonne said, "probably not." But she didn't sound too convincing.

Rick leaned back in his chair, one eye on the Gavin trade magazine charts, as he and Yvonne went over which songs to add or drop from the play list next week. "Where's your shadow today?" he asked, keeping his tone casual. It was the first day in a week that Christie hadn't been at the station by early afternoon.

"I told her you and I were going over the music right after I got off the air," Yvonne said. "She said she'd be in later."

"Doesn't she *ever* sleep?" It sounded more impatient than he'd intended.

Rick wasn't sure what Christie's frequent visits

were doing to her sleep schedule, but they weren't doing anything for his concentration. He kept getting distracted by the sound of female laughter from Yvonne's office across the hall. If Christie had been getting in the way, the problem would be easy to solve. But she was making herself useful, taking some of the weight off Yvonne's shoulders. She was willing to help with anything—filing, organizing tapes and CDs, or helping to pack up the van for a live remote broadcast. All further proof that Rick had made a good call when he hired her.

Yvonne was studying him. "What is it with you and her, anyway?"

"I don't know what you're talking about." His answer came out a little too quickly.

"Do you have some kind of problem with her?"

Rick raised an eyebrow. "Aside from the two of you gabbing across the hall like magpies, no. I don't have a problem with her. Why?"

The problem was, he found her just about impossible to ignore. Try as he might. When she wasn't in Yvonne's office, she was up and down the hall on one errand or another, usually singing some snatch of a song. Often, it was the one that was on the air; just as often, it could be some obscure country song or show tune. Not that she was too loud; in fact, the singing always got quieter as she went by his door, and always picked up again when she passed it. Well, no wonder. He'd been all but rude to her, and there was no good reason for it. He could shut his door, but that would be the final act of defeat. In five years as program director here, he'd made it a point to always keep it open, always be available.

"You've barely said two words to the girl since she got here," Yvonne said. "And why in the world were you monitoring her first air shift? You probably scared her half to death."

"The CD player jammed, and I bailed her out. She *complained* about that?" Rick caught himself raising his voice.

"No." Yvonne backed off. "She just told me about the problem with the player, and she said you called."

"I told her she was doing a good job. Did she tell you that?"

"She didn't really say anything." Yvonne was still backpedalling. "I was just surprised you'd be listening at that hour. Especially her first night. You know everybody's first shift is usually awful."

"I was *helping*."

Yvonne held her hands up in front of her in a gesture of defense. "I know, I know."

"So why am I a beast all of a sudden?" His voice had risen again.

She didn't bat an eye. "I don't know, Rick. Why *are* you a beast all of a sudden?"

A silence followed. What was happening to him? He never yelled at the jocks. If one of them needed to be chewed out, which was rare, his voice got deadly quiet. It was much more effective. He wasn't sure if Yvonne needed chewing out—she never had before—but something had to be done, and quick. "Sorry," he said. "I guess I need some more sleep. Or more coffee."

"I'd lay off the caffeine if I were you," Yvonne said.

This had gone far enough. He and Yvonne had always had a good working relationship. They'd even done some friendly flirting. It was safe, because both of them knew it didn't mean anything. That had stopped cold the day Christie had heard him call Yvonne "gorgeous" over the phone. He felt as if he'd just been caught. Caught at nothing.

And now, Yvonne was starting to overstep her bounds. Time to get things back under control. "Are you finished?" he said.

"Well, there is one more thing."

Rick refused to cringe as he waited for the other shoe to drop.

"Well, she wants to learn everything. And she's sharp as a tack, Rick. I don't know if you—"

He circled his hand in the air, motioning for her to speed up. "Yes, I've noticed. Your point is—?"

"One of the things she's interested in is the music. She was here the other day when I was listening to some of the new discs—the songs you're thinking about adding to the play list—"

"Right."

"Well, she might be asking you about adding a segment on her show where she auditions a couple of new songs and gets the listeners' opinions."

Rick groaned and dropped his head against the back of his chair.

"Now, I'm not trying to tell you what to decide—"

"I should hope not."

"Just—be nice, Rick. Okay?"

He brought his head up, looked her in the eye and said, with perfect blandness, "I'm always nice."

Christie finally decided to approach Rick about the new music segment after he was off the air, since she knew he usually didn't go home right away. She'd been stalling, balking at another encounter in the office she still thought of as the lion's den. And at the thought of making a fool of herself. She hadn't been within six feet of him in the past two weeks, and even at that distance, he set her off balance. Enough was enough. She needed to prove to Rick, as well as herself, that she could hold a conversation with him without being intimidated, or succumbing to ridiculous little butterflies. She had to make sure he knew she had a brain in her head.

When she arrived at the station shortly after 7 P.M., the production room door was closed, with the light above it glowing bright red, indicating the microphone was in use. *Cutting commercials. Of course.*

She'd come to attack the beach at Normandy, and the Germans were out to lunch.

Christie headed to the break room to wait him out, rounded the corner, and walked straight into Rick. He was turning away from the coffee machine, mug in hand.

Before she knew what was happening, Rick caught her around the shoulders with his free arm and spun her neatly around in a half-circle. All she could see was Rick's crisp white shirt up against her face. All she could feel were his arm and his chest, both warm and firm, with Christie captured in the middle. Then she came to a stop, and Rick reached past her to set his sloshing coffee cup on the counter.

He pulled her back and steadied her with both hands. "Are you okay?"

His hands on her shoulders felt as warm and firm as the rest of him. Christie staggered back. He held her by the elbows, still steadying her.

"I'm sorry," he said. "Did I get you?"

One brief little spin couldn't account for her light-headedness, or the sudden speed of her heart. Christie looked down at the splashed coffee, in a semicircle pattern on the floor around them. "How did you do that?"

"I'm not sure." He laughed. "Reflexes took over. Did I spill any on you?"

He studied her, his hands still on her shoulders, and for a second Christie could imagine he was searching for something other than spilled coffee. Then he let her go and stepped back.

She reached her arms up around herself, self-consciously patting down her sweater. "I don't think so." She was still catching her breath. "I thought you were in the production room."

"Just on my way back to it. What are you doing here this time of night?"

This wasn't how she'd planned on approaching him. Their first real, face-to-face contact since she'd started, and it was a head-on collision. "I—" She couldn't think. "I wanted to run something by you. If you have time." She brushed a strand of hair back from her face. "And I thought I'd mop up some coffee."

"It's a deal." Rick moved toward the hallway, but

his eyes were locked on hers. Was there a little unease on his side, too? "I've just got one commercial left to cut. Meet me in my office in ten minutes?"

Christie used the ten minutes to take care of the spill as best she could with paper towels, while she got her heart to slow down. Just shaken up, she told herself, although getting whirled around by Rick had been more enjoyable than she cared to think about. *I need to get out more.*

At least he seemed to be in a good mood. And his shirt had smelled good.

The break room floor's thin carpet bore plenty of evidence of past spills. When Christie was satisfied that the latest splatters weren't any worse than the others, she went to Rick's office. He'd beaten her there, and she wondered how long it would be before she could whip out a commercial in less than ten minutes.

Christie had a sense of déjà vu as she sat down, once again, in "The Chair." She tried to forget that crashing into him had been like running into a warm wall.

A warm wall. It wasn't a bad description. Rick wasn't exactly cold, but he wasn't exactly approachable either. He leaned back again in the big chair as he listened to her. His posture was deceptively relaxed, but the watchful gray eyes told her otherwise. It was hard to read those eyes as she described what she had in mind: audition a couple of songs a night and take calls from the listeners. She would get their reactions—anything from a simple tally of which song they preferred, to more detailed comments, if they had any. It seemed, to her, like a good way to get a sense of what the listeners would like to hear on the station.

The idea was simple enough. Maybe he'd thought of it before. Maybe that was why he showed almost no expression until she finished.

"Christie—" he said when she was done. He fingered the handle of the omnipresent black coffee cup, and sighed. "Time for a lesson in Ugly Radio Reality."

She had the feeling he'd be able to mop her up like so much spilled coffee by the time this was over.

Rick tried not to notice the vulnerable look on her face, or the way her light green sweater brought out the burnished shades of her hair. He cleared his throat.

"Radio stations," he said, "are programmed a certain way. We actually have more freedom here than they do in Los Angeles. There, it's all done by consultants. The program director gets the play list—boom. Done. That's why those L.A. stations have that uniform sound."

"With the same few songs. It drives me nuts."

"But it works. The ugly truth is, people *want* to hear the familiar. They'll say they want more variety, but if they hear something they don't know, their first urge is to change the station. Which is exactly what we don't want them to do."

"You're saying new songs scare people away?" The idea visibly incensed her.

Rick nodded. "I don't like it any better than you do. But it's true."

"So that's why most of what we play is at least ten years old."

"You got it."

Christie moved forward slightly in her chair, her hair just brushing the shoulders of the soft-looking sweater. "But we do add new songs eventually."

"And ever so carefully."

"So what's wrong with me prescreening a couple? Wouldn't that help give you an idea which songs the listeners are more receptive to?"

Her eyes were full of purpose, and hope. Yvonne was right. Christie was sharp. But it was her determination that would take her far. Unfortunately, all that ambition had to be tempered with reality. And he had the dirty job of dishing it out.

"We have the trade magazines for that. And—"

"And?"

With another deep sigh, he leaned back in his chair, reluctantly meeting her eyes as he prepared to give her another dose of disillusionment. "Ugly Radio Truth Number Two. Have you noticed what kind of listeners call on your shift?"

Rick watched her wince, and knew he'd hit home. The overnight audience consisted largely of drunks, depressed people with no lives, and a lot more who were just plain—strange. "Overnight listeners are a different breed. They're not really. . .representative of our main audience."

"So what are overnights for?" She didn't quite hide the frustration in her voice, but it was a good try.

He looked at the pretty redhead perched on the chair in front of him. No wonder he'd avoided her. She was a fascinating mix of determination and vulnerability. He admired the determination, but the vulnerability killed him.

That wouldn't do. He collected his thoughts and dealt the final blow.

"Overnights? They're life support for the station," he answered flatly. "Radio is a twenty-four hour business, so we need a live body on the premises twenty-four hours a day. It's also a place where advertisers can buy commercial time at inexpensive rates. And, of course, if there's ever a fire or flood, we're the local Emergency Alert station."

"So I'm here in case of a disaster." Christie maintained eye contact, but her glassy look struck right at the center of Rick's conscience. He'd been way too blunt. There was a difference between being realistic and being sadistic.

Rick contemplated her steadily, and his voice softened. "No. It's also a place where talented newcomers can sharpen their craft. Make all those beginner's mistakes in front of a smaller audience. It's a starting point."

Christie thought she was beginning to read his expression, and it looked suspiciously like compassion. Just what she didn't want. She scraped up her remaining dignity and stood.

"Okay," she said. "Fair enough." She faked a smile. "It doesn't hurt to ask, right?"

Rick stood, too. Another display of gentlemanly manners. "No, it doesn't hurt to ask." He looked as if he were going to say something more. For no good reason, Christie flashed back to the way he'd steadied her after their crash in the break room. Yet for the most part, it seemed his mission in life was to cut her off at the knees.

He was talking again, something about not needing to set the world on fire her first month. She didn't want to hear it. All she wanted was to get out of there.

She didn't need anyone to feel sorry for her. She could do it herself, thank you very much. She hurried out to find a place where she could do just that, in private.

Rick returned to the production room to record the commercial he'd been too tongue-tied to finish after his collision with Christie. This time he did it in one take, but his mind was elsewhere.

He'd given his troublesome rookie her first disappointment. Well, at least she hadn't taken it out on him, although he could tell she'd been tempted. She'd put a good face on, the way professionals were supposed to do. And he'd given her the right answer, the same answer he would have given any other jock. He wasn't any harder on Christie than he was on anyone else.

Was he?

Hard to say. No one else had approached him about anything similar. Rob had his requests and dedications. Yvonne did a noon feature on Fridays, one hour that he let her have free rein with. Of course, Yvonne had more experience.

Okay, so Christie's idea, kept within limits, wouldn't have hurt anything. Major-market stations weren't as flexible as this one. He'd given her a realistic idea of what she could expect somewhere else.

He loaded the commercial into the computer and went back to his office for his jacket. Picking it up from the back of his chair, he looked up to see Christie framed in the doorway. If it was possible, she looked more crestfallen than she had a few minutes ago.

She said, "Do you have jumper cables?"

Chapter Four

Rick almost laughed. He understood the look on Christie's face perfectly. It was such a clear-cut case of adding insult to injury.

"I tried Rob first," she added.

I'm sure you did, he thought. "Wouldn't have worked anyway. I don't think we have a song long enough for him to get clear over to the parking structure and jump a car." Rick picked up his keys. "It's okay, I've got cables. Let's go."

Christie led him out, and Rick noticed again how straight her posture was when her pride was wounded. "Thanks," the back of her head said to him. "I thought it was starting a little funny, but. . ." she trailed off.

"I've been there. Everyone has."

That did it for conversation until Rick drove them to Christie's car. Her Toyota had to be fifteen years old if it was a day. It was a bright shade of blue rarely seen on the road these days. A typical car for a disc jockey, but not for a loan processor. Rick suddenly felt something akin to embarrassment over his car, a three-year-old sedan he'd bought just last year. Up until he'd financially recovered from the divorce, he'd driven a car much like Christie's. But she didn't know that.

He'd barely stopped before she scrambled out of his car. Rick caught up with her as she was starting to open the hood of her old Toyota. "I can get it," he said.

"The latch is tricky," she said, groping underneath the hood. When she pulled it up, he was surprised at what he saw. He didn't know much about cars, but the parts inside lacked the look of age and grime he'd expected. "How old is this car?"

"It's an '85. I bought it used when I was seventeen."

"Looks like you've taken pretty good care of it."

"It didn't look like this when I bought it. I paid for the car, but my dad did all the work."

There was something final-sounding about her use of the past tense. Rick looked at Christie, but her eyes were on the engine. The car would never be a classic, but it clearly meant something to her. He wanted to ask, but something stopped him. Instead, he got the cables and hooked up the cars. By the time the Toyota roared to life, the obvious had occurred to him.

Without disconnecting the jumper cables, he went to Christie's window on the driver's side. "We have a problem here," he said. "Where do you go now?"

"Why?" There was a hint of challenge in her tone. Rick could imagine what she was thinking: *as far away from you as possible.*

He rested his hand on the door. "We don't know if your battery's even charging. You could lose your headlights, maybe lose power altogether. There's no telling if you'd make it home or not." He sighed. Letting Christie out on the road, no matter how badly she wanted to go, just wasn't an option. And she was supposed to be on the air in a few hours. This was getting complicated. "You shouldn't be driving this car at all. Not until you get it checked."

He was glad the two cars were still attached by the cables. If Christie could have pulled away, he was sure she would have. It was a good thing she was reasonable enough not to drive off, cables and all. His ex-wife might have.

Christie's voice sounded carefully neutral. "What do you suggest?"

"I know a good repair shop in town. We can leave your car there, drop a key through the slot in the door and have them working on it tomorrow morning." Silence. He reiterated, "You can't drive this car over the hill. It's not safe."

Her hands were clenched on the wheel. "So how do I—"

Here was where it got tricky. "Well," he said, "I, for one, think better on a full stomach. Why don't we get a bite to eat?"

Silence. Except for the two cars idling in the background.

"Look," he said. "I know this is awkward. But I'm starved, and it'll give us a chance to sort this out."

Christie looked at him directly for the first time since this debacle started. Those pretty hazel eyes were still full of frustration, but at least not all of it seemed to be directed at him. "Rick, you don't have to do this."

He couldn't always read women very well, but at the moment, Christie was coming in loud and clear. She was stranded, a damsel in distress. And it galled the heck out of her.

He respected that need for independence, but somehow, it made him want to take care of her, too. A little warning bell sounded in the back of Rick's mind. He ignored it for the moment. The situation was getting touchy, but there were certain things he just wouldn't do. Leaving Christie stuck in an untrustworthy car was one of them.

"Look at it this way," he told her. "I was about to go home to microwave dinner-in-a-box. *You're* rescuing *me.*"

"But. . ." She was running out of arguments.

"Besides," he said, "I've never known a woman yet who could resist Chinese food." He knew of a place nearby. It was brightly lit, and platonic.

At last, Christie relented. "Okay."

The restaurant was just a few blocks from the station and looked as if it had been there for at least twenty years. Most of the tables were empty, not surprisingly; it was a quarter to nine. By Christie's calculations, she had a little over two hours to fill before she could reasonably escape back to the station to do her commercials, and then her air shift.

She was still smarting from the meeting in Rick's office. Now she was also squirming over the new situation she found herself in. The drive to the restaurant, at least, had been fairly painless. It seemed as if the farther Rick got from the station, the less—well, managerial—he became. But Christie couldn't afford to forget he was the boss. This night had already taken enough twists as it was.

"I imagine they'll have your car ready by early afternoon," Rick said as the waitress brought their food. "I'll give Sid a call in the morning."

"You know them there?"

He grinned. "Intimately." He spooned rice onto his plate. "You should have seen what I was driving a year ago. I was over there almost every other week. I practically had my own parking space."

"Really?"

"Oh, yeah. But the car I drove when I first started in radio was worse." He shook his head, pleasant crinkles showing at the corners of his eyes. "The ugliest green rust bucket you ever saw."

Christie looked up from her cashew chicken, intrigued. It was hard to imagine this was the same man who'd trashed her idea so soundly a little while ago. His whole demeanor had warmed up about ten degrees sometime in the last hour. She had the feeling of some door being opened a little crack, and decided to try for a peek inside. "How *did* you get started in radio?"

"You could say I stumbled in." Rick gave the contents of his plate a light dousing of soy sauce. "I was in college. A music major. But for one of my electives, I signed up for the school paper. One of my first assignments was a story on the campus radio station. I wound up quitting the paper and joining the station.

A year later, I got a full-time gig in Fresno and quit school." His smile glinted across the table, and he nodded at her. "Overnights."

"You left college to do overnights in Fresno?" It didn't fit her impression of him. He was too straight-laced, too well-ordered. The only male at the station, outside of sales or upper management, who wore shirts that buttoned down the front.

He nodded. "I told you, it's an addiction. There was no reasoning with me. For actors, they say it's the smell of greasepaint. For me, I guess it was the music and the microphone."

"So how long did it take before you were doing nights in L.A.?"

Rick's fork stopped halfway to his mouth. His eyes shifted away, as if he'd been caught at something. "How did you know that?"

"I heard you. I went to UCLA."

"And you remembered?" He looked flattered, she thought, and a little self-conscious. Then a new expression crossed his face—one of mock horror. "And you were still in *college?*" He clutched at his chest. "Oh, the pain."

"What's the big deal? That was only—" she hesitated—"five or six years ago."

Rick narrowed his eyes at her. "You're not making it any better."

"Oh, come on! How old would you have been then?"

"Watch it," he warned.

"I'd say right now you're about—"

"Careful," he said. "No buttering up the boss."

Uh-oh. Now she didn't dare guess too low. She took a guess and added a year for credibility. "Thirty-four?"

"Thirty-three," he shot back, then grinned. "Anyway, I don't think it's legal for you to ask me that."

Christie did the math. He was seven years older than she was. Or, six years and change. Not that it mattered. "So, when you were in L.A., you were about twenty-eight. Two years older than me." She poked at her food. "I've got some catching up to do."

"Watch out for that brass ring," he said. "When you're aiming for that, it's easy to fall."

She met his eyes. He didn't seem to be joking. She'd wandered very close to something here, and she wasn't sure how hard to press. Curiosity won out. "What happened? You disappeared somewhere during my junior year."

His glance drifted away. Long, slim fingers ran up and down the side of his water glass. "I disappeared, all right."

She'd stepped on shaky ground. "Oh. Was that when . . ."

"When the marriage blew up," he said matter-of-factly. "I dropped off the radar for about a year after that." He ran a hand through his hair and straightened in his chair. Christie sensed that door closing. "Then I came here. Happy ending." He slapped his hand on the tabletop, as if to adjourn the subject. "Now, you, I'm still trying to figure out."

"What do you mean?"

"Well, for one thing, you finished college, unlike me. And you seem sane enough. What made you want to go into radio?"

Back to that again. This time it wasn't a job interview question, but Christie still found she had to watch her answer. He didn't need to know what a mouse she'd been, or how invisible she'd felt. Six-foot-two males never needed to worry about disappearing. She bit her lip. "Well, if you stumbled in, I guess I groped my way in. I told you before, the loan business bored me to tears. I wanted something I could care about, and I've always loved music."

"I noticed. You're always singing up and down the hall like the happy sailors in one of those old MGM movies."

She felt herself blush. "I try to keep it down."

"I know. That makes it worse." Rick's eyes gleamed. "You walk past my door, I miss a line, and for the rest of the day I've got a song in my head I can't figure out. You *know* that's torture." She laughed at his mock exasperation. She'd known he had a sense of humor, but usually it was dry and acerbic. He'd lightened somehow tonight, and Christie found it dangerously appealing. "I never know *what* I'm going to hear out of you," he said. "What in the world do you listen to at home?"

"Oh, rock 'n' roll, rhythm and blues, country, Frank Sinatra, a little classical. Stuff like that."

"Stuff like that," he echoed.

"And current music, too. But that, I can get in my car."

He was contemplating her with one of those hard-to-read looks. "Wherever you go, make sure they know you like a broad base of music. It could keep you alive if there's a format change. That, and your production skills."

Christie flinched inwardly. She didn't like to hear him talk about her *going* anywhere.

The high-pitched ring of a cellular phone interrupted them, and Rick fished in the pocket of his jacket. Christie hadn't realized he carried a cell phone. She listened with growing suspicion as he took the call. Most of his answers were monosyllabic, but she was getting the gist of it.

"Okay, thanks anyway," he said. "I'll try you next time."

Rick flipped his cell phone shut, took one look at Christie's face, and got ready for the coming argument. He knew he'd postponed it as long as he could.

"What was that about?" she asked.

"One of our part-timers," he said casually, pocketing the phone. "I did some calling around after we ordered, trying to get hold of someone to fill your shift tonight."

Here it came. Part two of the debate that had started in the parking structure. "Rick, you don't have to do that. I'm already here."

"No, think about it." Rick tried once more to make her see reason. "I can drop you off at the station. But who's going to run you home at 6 A.M.? I can take you after we're done with dinner, and you can get a ride back during the day tomorrow, after your car's ready."

He'd expected her to argue. He hadn't expected her to look as if he'd offered to give her a root canal using his own personal power tools. "No," she said. "I can work tonight. I'll get a ride in the morning." Christie frowned. "Where did you make the calls, anyway? From the men's room?"

"No, I stepped outside."

"Why?"

"For some reason, I thought you might argue with me about it."

"You were right."

"I see that. But seriously. What are you going to do?"

She bit her lip. "I've got a neighbor across the hall. I'll call in the morning, around seven, and ask her to pick me up. She's always around town on sales calls. She'll be able to work me in."

"That still leaves you stuck for at least two hours." He wasn't comfortable with it, but he was also aware that his phone wasn't ringing. Without a substitute for her shift tonight, the whole discussion would be irrelevant anyway.

"It's okay," she said. "Really. You've been too nice already."

"Too nice?" He gave up and shook his head. "You must have me confused with someone else."

None of the part-timers materialized to fill in for Christie at the last minute, so Rick resigned himself to that lost battle. Instead, they moved on to Starbuck's for coffee when the Chinese restaurant closed at ten. Another hour went by rapidly, filled with talk that moved on from music to life in general. In spite of its awkward beginning, he couldn't remember enjoying an evening so much in a long time. Before he knew it, it was time to take Christie to the station.

There was no need to bother with the parking structure this time. Rick pulled up to the curb across from the entrance to the studio. He shut off the engine, ready to walk her to the door, but she stopped him. "You don't have to get out. It's right over there."

He supposed she was right. It wasn't like this was a date, after all. At least it shouldn't be.

But she wasn't getting out yet, and it was getting harder to remember just where this relationship was supposed to leave off. Did she feel it too? If she did, they were both in trouble. Christie smiled, her hand resting on the door. A safety latch? "Rick—this was nice of you. Really. Thanks."

"No problem." It would have been the most natural thing in the world to reach over, put his arm around her, even just squeeze her hand. But company policy frowned on doing what came naturally, at least with employees. It was a policy Rick had always agreed with. So he kept both hands on the steering wheel.

"See you tomorrow." Christie pulled the handle on the door, on her way to spend several hours alone in an empty building.

Before she could get out, he said, "Christie?"

She turned back, and their eyes met under the car's interior dome light. Rick silently sucked in his breath. "About overnights. Don't worry about what I said. No one does them for too long."

"You said there wasn't much turnover here," she reminded him.

"Which means one of these days you'll bail out on

me." He said it lightly, but he didn't like the taste of the words. "Or, after you've been here long enough, Rob could get hit by a bus."

She laughed, then added hastily, "Don't say that. I don't want to wish anything bad on anybody." Christie glanced at the window of the studio, where Rob was. "Maybe his rich uncle could die and leave him a fortune."

"Oh? Pretty tough on the uncle."

She tilted her head, as though considering. "His rich, *evil* uncle."

He laughed, and then she was out of the car.

Christie couldn't shake a pleasant, lighthearted feeling as she walked into the studio. At the sight of Rob, she had a hard time keeping a straight face. She should tell him to watch out for buses. In spite of her efforts, a smile cracked through.

Rob saw it. "Okay. What's so funny?"

"Nothing." Christie moved past him as they traded sides of the counter.

"Uh-oh." Rob bent down to peer at her face. "If you say 'nothing,' it must be me. What is it? Spaghetti on my shirt? Toilet paper on my shoe?"

She shook her head and waved him away.

"Laughing at me," he muttered in feigned paranoia. "I knew it all along. If you weren't so pretty—"

"You'd what?" she challenged him. In the past few weeks, getting hit on by Rob had become as much a part of her night as plugging in her headphones. But he was too good-natured to be offensive, and there was no pressure behind it. "Tell me the truth, Rob. If I

ever came after you, I'll bet you'd run away screaming."

He propped his hands on the counter and leaned
over the control board. "Try me."

Maybe in high school. Not now. "Dream on." A
light bulb of inspiration flashed in Christie's mind. A
way of answering a question she didn't dare ask out-
right. "It's probably against company policy, anyway."

"Only if I was your supervisor. Or the other way
around." He opened the door to leave. "So watch out."

After Rob left, Christie stared at the window blinds.
In her mind, she saw past the window, to the curb
where Rick's car had pulled away a few minutes ago.

That answered *that* question.

Chapter Five

"I just don't know what I'm doing wrong," Christie said to Yvonne. "I try so hard to catch his eye, but he just doesn't seem to notice me any more."

"I know how you feel," Yvonne said. "I had the same problem with my boyfriend a few months ago. Our romance was going nowhere! Then I went to the beauty experts at Sensational Salon, and they gave me a total makeover." A smug giggle. "He's been all over me ever since."

"Shensational—oh, rats, I did it again." Christie dropped the commercial script to her side with an exasperated sigh. "Sorry, I keep tripping over the name. Who wrote this schlock, anyway?"

Standing in front of the production room's other microphone, Yvonne rolled her eyes in agreement. "Sales rep, probably. Or worse, the owner of the business."

"Sensational Salon." Christie forced her mouth

around it, one syllable at a time. "I hope no one I know ever hears this."

"It could be worse. I did a commercial one time for some PMS remedy." Yvonne turned back to the microphone and said brightly: "Hi! My name is Yvonne Reyes, and I used to kill people on a monthly basis."

Christie laughed. "Hi!" she chirped into her own microphone. "My name is Christie Becker, and I used to be a hag."

Both of them broke down laughing, and the production room door opened. Rick leaned halfway in, his hand still on the doorknob. "Yvonne," he said, not waiting for their laughter to subside. Yvonne pulled her headphones down around her neck. "You've still got music logs to do, right?"

"Right."

Rick turned to Christie. "I'm shorthanded on news. Can I see you in the studio as soon as you're done recording this spot?"

Christie's eyes widened in alarm. She gave the only answer she could under the circumstances: "Sure."

Rick was gone, and the door closed behind him, before she could say anything else.

Yvonne stared at the door. "I wonder what happened to Jonathan."

Jonathan Blair did the morning and late afternoon newscasts, as well as a two-hour air shift to fill the gap between Yvonne and Rick. "It must have been fast," Christie said. "He was on the air an hour ago." She held a hand to her suddenly-clenched stomach. "Oh, boy."

"You okay?" Yvonne studied her. "They taught you news at broadcasting school, right?"

"A couple of hours worth of class time. It's been a while."

"I've never seen you this nervous."

Christie grimaced. "You've never seen me when I'm about to talk for three minutes straight. In front of Rick."

"You'll do fine. He doesn't bite. Haven't you figured that out yet?"

Christie smiled weakly. Her dealings with Rick were more relaxed since he'd rescued her last week, but the thought of doing the news in front of him still rattled her. For this job, she would have cheerfully agreed to juggle knives. It was just her luck that Rick needed her, at a moment's notice, to do something she had almost no training in.

She finished recording the hideous commercial with Yvonne, then went off to the studio to meet her fate.

"Emergency?" she asked Rick, trying to borrow some of the phony cheer from the commercial she'd just finished cutting.

"And how." Rick circled the counter and led her down the hall. As they passed the production room, he leaned in once more, barely breaking his stride. "Yvonne? Cue the next couple of songs for me in the studio, okay?"

Christie could only assume Yvonne nodded. There wasn't any time to glance into the production room as Rick herded her down the hall. "I'm going to have to run through this really quick," he told her. "The first news break is twenty-five minutes from now. Nothing like a little pressure, huh?"

He led her into the tiny newsroom that neighbored the studio. There was barely enough room for the desk, which was crowded with a computer, printer and telephone. A microphone was mounted onto the edge of the desk. "You won't be using that," Rick said. "It's been dead for I don't know how long. We do the news from the guest microphone in the studio. It works better if we're face-to-face anyway."

Christie gulped. She'd never have a better chance to screw up.

Rick pulled back the rolling chair for her to sit in front of the computer. This time, it was more like a silent order than a gentlemanly gesture. Christie sat. "You've heard the old expression 'rip and read,' from the old teletype machines?" He reached over her shoulder to operate the computer mouse. "These days, it's 'print and read.' "

Rick leaned over her, his head just above hers as he explained where to find the news stories on the Internet, and how to turn them into radio copy. Christie stared at the computer screen and concentrated fiercely. For a moment, Rick rested his hand on her shoulder; the next moment, he lifted it away, never pausing as he spoke. It was as if it had never been there at all.

Rick finished sketching out her instructions, then straightened. "Got it?" Christie nodded, trying not to look dazed. She must not have succeeded completely. He bent down again, bringing his eyes level with hers.

"Listen, I know you're going into this cold. Just do what you can."

In nineteen minutes, Christie added to herself as Rick left. She wasted a moment staring at the clock on the room's gray acoustic-carpeted wall, then shook herself. No time to worry about how little time she had. No time for sorting out the butterflies in her stomach. Certainly no time to get worked up over a little touch from the boss. She turned her attention to the computer screen and concentrated on the headlines with all her might.

Christie did her first newscast in a near-trance, focusing studiously on the words on the paper in front of her. But a part of her couldn't forget the gray eyes she felt watching her from the other side of those pages. Despite her concentration, when it was over, she couldn't remember a thing she'd just said.

She looked up at Rick; he was nodding in satisfaction. "Not bad," he said. Christie pursed her lips to silence the sigh of relief that whooshed out of her. Rick started putting away a stack of CDs, damage control for the clutter that had accumulated in the studio during the first hour of his shift. "I'll need you back in here at five-thirty. Do you have any problem staying through the six-thirty news?"

"No."

He glanced up from sorting and shelving. "Thanks." His smile was brief, but it was genuine. She must have done all right.

An hour later, when she finished her six o'clock newscast, the heat was off. Just one more to go, and she had enough material to work with now. The studio seemed a little less frenetic at the moment, so she asked, "What happened to Jonathan?"

"Family emergency. He got a call after I went on the air. His grandmother back east had a stroke. I sent him out so he could catch a flight." By his tone, she could tell it wouldn't have occurred to him to do otherwise. Christie wasn't sure her old employers would have been so accommodating.

The phone light flashed, and Rick turned to answer it. While he did, Christie lingered a moment to take in the controlled chaos around her. She'd been working here almost a month now, but this was the first time she'd seen Rick in the studio.

What she saw was a man in his element.

Rick's studio was physically the same room she worked in night after night, but apart from that, it was a different world. The afternoon drive shift buzzed with activity. Phone lights flashed, bringing in traffic reports and listeners' requests. Newspapers, trade magazines and scratch paper with various notes covered every surface. And at the center of all this chaos was Rick—often intently focused, but never seeming rattled, even when he was doing five things at once. He always seemed to know which direction to turn to find the needed scrap of paper amid the layers that were strewn around. If she ran this show for even half an hour, Christie thought, she wouldn't remember her own name.

As she watched, Rick recorded another phone call, cued a CD, and jotted an apparently unrelated note on another scrap of paper. She couldn't help admiring his seeming ease: quick, but never rushed; intent, but never stressed. No wasted motion. She didn't think he noticed when she slipped out.

But he was waiting to greet her when she came in for her final newscast at six-thirty. "Last one," Rick said. "Stay on the air with me after you finish your stories this time."

"What?" Just when she thought it was safe.

"No big deal," he said, putting on his headphones. "Just stay loose, and we'll talk before I start the next song."

Rick introduced the traffic, then the news; there was no time for her to think about it. Probably just the way he'd planned.

She finished the newscast with her two biggest stumbles of the day. When it was over, Rick said, "Now, in case you've been wondering just who you've been hearing on the news this afternoon—" he met her eyes, giving her a nod across the console "— Christie Becker, our overnight personality, filling in for Jonathan Blair on very short notice." He fired off an applause sound effect.

She felt a twinge of embarrassment and put it to use. "Please. You're making me blush."

"They can't see you blush." He grinned. "Remember, this is radio."

To her surprise, her nerves faded under his smile. "This is radio?" She smacked at her forehead. "That explains the microphone."

"And the fact that neither of us have gotten paid in a month," Rick added.

"*And* the fact that we're both dumb enough to keep doing it."

Rick laughed. *"Touché."* He started the music, then straightened away from the microphone, pulling down his headphones. "Very nice."

"Fun," Christie agreed, returning his grin. It may not have been hilarious, but it had been spontaneous. It had *felt* good. Best of all, she hadn't fallen on her face.

They were both still smiling when Rick met her eyes, and Christie felt something.

Click.

Professional chemistry? Or something else?

Christie stepped backward, and bumped into the wall behind her. "Am I done?"

"Just a minute." He was still looking at her, but his expression had changed to one of thoughtful assessment. Probably for some purely professional reason. A brief frown passed over his brow, then faded. "How'd you like to do it for the rest of the week?"

Just as she'd suspected. Purely professional. Christie leaned back, borrowing a little support from the wall. "News?"

Rick nodded. "Jonathan won't be back in until next Monday, at least. I'll need someone to fill in." He nodded again, as though agreeing with himself. "This worked out fine. You did a nice job. There's a difference between reading news and commercials. You know the difference. And the last break—" He shrugged. "I think we play off each other pretty well."

She folded her arms. "Always a method to your madness, isn't there?"

"Usually." He didn't bother to hide a smile. "You'd have to do the morning news, too. And that two-hour air shift from two to four in the afternoon, between Yvonne's and mine. It's a weird schedule, but it all adds up to about eight hours, if you do it right. And your day starts at about 5:30 A.M., so I'll want you to do it right. Which means no volunteering for Yvonne while you're doing this. You get some rest between the morning news and your afternoon shift. Can you do that?" He seemed to realize she hadn't said yes yet. "And are you interested?"

A week in the studio with Rick. It appealed to her for more than just professional reasons, and that was the problem. Christie thought for a moment, but there was really nothing to think about. Any new challenge was a vote of confidence, and she'd be a fool to turn it down. Especially a chance to be on the air in broad daylight.

So she said what she should have said in the first place. "Sure."

"You'll have to put up with McKeon on the morning shift. Let me know if he gives you too much trouble." The matter settled, Rick started shelving CDs again. "Of course, I hear that afternoon drive guy's even worse."

Two days later, Rick drummed out a song intro on the black countertop. Christie entered the studio with her clipboard of news stories and took her place across the counter from him. As she checked over the papers in front of her, she started singing along with the music, without any apparent break in her concentration. That didn't surprise Rick at this point; she seemed to know the words to everything. The girl must breathe music.

A few days ago, she never would have started singing in front of him so easily. Rick was tempted to tease her, but he didn't.

Christie jotted a change on her news copy and glanced up, breaking off the song for the first time. "You get more upbeat songs on this shift."

"It's called day-parting. Wouldn't want to keep your overnight audience awake."

She fixed him with a mock glare, and he grinned at her. He was going to miss her when she went back to her regular schedule. He'd been putting Christie on the air with him for more and more of his breaks as the week wore on, rather than just when they were going into the news. It was fun, and it added to the show. He and Jonathan worked together smoothly, but it wasn't like this.

"Rick?" He inclined his head, prompting her to go on. "Would you mind if I slipped out a little early tonight, after the last newscast?"

That was as late as he officially needed her to stay, anyway. He could spare her for the last half hour. "Sure." Rick picked up the log to sign off on the previous hour. He kept his eyes on the page as he scrawled his initials. "Date?" he asked her. He made the single syllable as casual as he could.

"A movie with Yvonne. It starts at seven." There was a pause. In an equally casual tone, she added, "You?"

Rick looked up from the log sheet. Christie's eyes were back on her news stories, checking over what

she'd already checked over. Her eyelashes were lowered in studied nonchalance, but she was biting her
lower lip, an enticing little habit that she probably
didn't know drove him crazy. Right there, on the
lower left corner. As if she were nibbling an appetizer
Rick would love to sample himself.

"Oh," he said, "you mean, do I have plans tonight?
Yes."

She looked up, and Rick caught a flicker in her eyes.
Gotcha.

He squinted up at the ceiling. "Let's see, tonight it's
. . . Budget Gourmet. Frozen beef medallions with
mushrooms."

She smiled, and her posture relaxed ever so slightly.
"I see. Does the veal parmigiana know about the beef
medallions?"

They both laughed.

"Want to use that, next break?" Christie asked.

"Sure." Rick had laid out two basic ground rules for
their on-air banter. One, he was never referred to as
the boss, he was just another hapless jock. Two, he
was fair game. In fact, if the jokes were on him, so
much the better. Rick pulled on his headphones and
got back to work, watching Christie as she did the
same.

He knew he was playing with fire. But it served her
right for biting her lip like that.

The week flew by.

Christie's mornings with Mark McKeon were every
bit as bad as Rick had warned. He was arrogant and
dismissive, never speaking to her on the air and rarely

at any other time. He obviously considered her news an interruption of his show; Christie wondered if he was any more civil to Jonathan.

The afternoons made up for it though. Being in the studio with Rick kept her on her toes in more ways than one, but she was learning. Their breaks together after the news kept getting better. No elaborate, scripted comedy bits, just simple, light banter. All things considered, Christie hated to see the week come to an end.

She was passing through the lobby on Friday, just before her two P.M. air shift, when a woman walked in the front door with a small boy. The receptionist wasn't up front, which wasn't unusual. At first, Christie had thought the girl was lazy, but that was before she found out how many other tasks Karen was pulled away from her desk to do.

Christie, in turn, had learned a thing or two about helping out at the front desk. "May I help you?"

"Is Rick here?" the woman said without preamble, and those three words brought the woman and boy into sharp focus.

She had never consciously tried to picture Rick's ex-wife, but somehow, this was just what Christie would have expected. She was tall, blonde and very pretty, with light blue eyes. At the moment she wore a preoccupied expression. The boy looked about six years old, with light brown hair. A dinosaur backpack hung loosely on his arm.

"Rick? He's out on a live appearance." Christie's clerical smile never deserted her. "Is there anything I can help you with?"

The blonde looked even more distracted. "When will he be back?"

Christie glanced at her watch, and remembered she was well aware what time it was: ten minutes before she was due to go on the air. "The remote ends at two, and it's just a few blocks away. I imagine about fifteen minutes."

"Oh." The woman put her hands on the little boy's shoulders. "I have to get back from my lunch break. Can I leave him with you?"

As if he were a UPS package, she thought. Christie's gaze shifted down to the solemn little face. Blue eyes, but darker than his mother's. "Would that be all right with you, hon?" Christie asked.

The boy shrugged. "Sure."

"Thank you." The former Mrs. Fox squeezed his small shoulder with a well-manicured hand and was quickly out the door.

Well, this was awkward. Christie glanced at her watch again, not surprised to find it was now eight minutes to two. She smiled at the boy. "Have a seat."

He plunked down on the fat brown cushions of the lobby couch, his short legs sticking out straight in front of him. He clutched a small action figure in his hand. Christie glanced down the hallway, but there was no sign of Karen's imminent return. If she didn't show up in the next few minutes, Christie decided, she'd take him into the studio with her. He seemed like a quiet little boy, and he'd probably been there before.

Rick had never even mentioned his son. What kind of a father was he?

"What's your name, honey?"

"Jason."

"Do you get to see your dad very often?"

The boy shrugged apathetically. "He's usually too busy."

Christie's opinion of Rick plummeted. She sat down on the couch beside Jason and turned her attention to the figure in his hands, a familiar green-faced monster. "That's a cool-looking Frankenstein monster there."

Jason turned his head toward her, noticeably more animated. "His name's not Frankenstein," he said authoritatively. "That's the doctor's name."

Christie nodded, trying to match his seriousness. "Of course. Everyone knows that."

The blue eyes got wider. "I've got a Wolfman, too," he said, reaching toward the floor for his backpack. "And a mummy . . ."

Within moments, Christie was admiring a collection of half a dozen miniature monsters. When she named each one correctly, Jason seemed impressed. "So," she said, "do you take these guys with you everywhere you go?"

Jason nodded. "I keep them on my nightstand at home." He lowered his voice. "But I have to make them face the other way before I go to sleep."

It was hard to keep a straight face, but Christie wouldn't make light of such a confession for the world. "I don't blame you. Monsters are cool, but I wouldn't want them staring at me at night, either."

The shy grin he gave her in response was irresistible. Then the glass front door swung open, and Jason's head snapped up.

"Uncle Rick!" The boy hurtled off the couch, and suddenly he was seven feet tall as Rick hoisted him up into his arms.

"Hey, bud!" Rick's grin was the most unreserved she'd seen on him yet.

And Christie felt like a heel. She stood up, watching the two a moment longer. She should head straight to the studio.

"You got here early," Rick was saying. "What happened?"

"Aunt Sylvia dropped me off on her lunch break. Mom wanted to take a nap at Aunt Sylvia's. She said it was a long drive, but I slept through most of it."

Christie found herself mentally sketching possible versions of the Fox family tree. *Aunt Sylvia* could be Rick's brother's wife. . . Or his sister. . .

Jason swung around in Rick's arms and pointed at Christie. "She knows all about monsters. She knows Frankenstein is the doctor's name!"

"Pretty smart for a girl," Rick conceded. He looked over at Christie. "Thanks for watching him."

"We're renting a monster movie tonight," Jason announced. The quiet, subdued little boy was gone, replaced by an armload of squirms. He twisted back to face Rick. "Can she come, too?"

Out of the mouths of babes.

Rick's eyes met hers, over Jason's shoulder, and they shared a moment of awkward hesitation. Through the silence that hung in the air, Christie could have sworn they were thinking the same thing.

They had a six-year-old chaperone. What could be safer?

Rick gave her a slight nod, and she smiled. "I'll bring the popcorn."

Chapter Six

Christie rang the bell of Rick's apartment and waited, her arm curled around a large bottle of cola. After working just a few feet across from him for a week, she shouldn't be nervous. It was no big deal. They were just friends. Increasingly good friends, over the past few days. But this was a new context, and one she wasn't sure she was ready for.

She didn't have long to prepare, because the door swung open, and there he was.

Not fair. He'd changed into jeans and a blue sweatshirt, the first time she'd seen him so casually dressed. His smile was relaxed, his thick brown hair slightly disheveled, and all traces of the boss were gone. It was that easy for men. Throw on some comfortable clothes, add an easy smile, and be transformed into serious hugging material.

Friends weren't supposed to look this good.

"Come on in," he said, stepping back. "The pizza's already here."

"Hi," she said, holding out the bottle of soda between them.

Rick took the bottle and closed the door. "Thanks." *Wait a minute. He'd shaved.* In the past week, Christie had gotten familiar with the light stubble that shadowed his face by the end of the day, and it was gone. That was little more effort than necessary, and the realization pleased her more than it should. She shouldn't *want* him to look nicer for her. She'd thought about driving home to change, but there wasn't really time, and a trip across the freeway would make it look like she was trying too hard.

This would be complicated enough if they were just playing a straight round of the dating game. But that was exactly what they were trying *not* to do.

Jason came to the rescue, popping his head over the back of the couch. "We got *two* pizzas!" he announced. "We usually just get one. Only one's got pineapples on it." He made a face.

"Ham and pineapple," Rick explained. "And the other one's pepperoni. I forgot to ask what you liked."

"Perfect." The scenario couldn't have been more natural. No candlelight seductions here; just two boys and a movie. So what if one of them was full-grown and gorgeous? Christie relaxed slightly, and held her plastic grocery bag aloft. "Microwave popcorn, as promised. Now, do you know the secret ingredient?"

"If you say diet butter spray I'm going to kill you."

"Just the opposite. M&Ms." He looked at her quizzically. Christie explained, "You throw them on as soon as the popcorn comes out of the microwave. They get all warm and melty on the inside." He still looked dubious. Just about everyone did, until they tried it. "Think about it. If you want to give it a try, I'll make a believer out of you."

Rick relieved her of the grocery bag and led her toward the kitchen, where two pizzas waited on the counter. While she helped herself to a slice of each, Christie glanced around Rick's apartment. No sign yet of any Christmas decorations, but then, it was only the first week of December. It was one of those apartments with no dividing wall or doorway between the living room and the kitchen; the carpet simply gave way to tile. A piano in the corner of the living room drew her eye. Incongruously, an exercise treadmill stood at the opposite end of the room.

She couldn't help herself. As he led her into the living room, she said, "Who decorated your place, Mozart or Gold's Gym?"

Rick laughed. "You know what they say. Out of sight, out of mind. I spend most of my time out here, and when the treadmill was in the bedroom, it was too easy to ignore. The piano—" He paused beside it, resting a hand on the keys to play a chord absently. It seemed as much an extension of him as the controls in the studio. He shrugged. "The piano belongs in the middle of the house."

Christie glanced at the sheet music resting on the music stand in front of the keys. It was an Andrew Lloyd Webber score. She would have loved to hear it, but she was sure Jason wouldn't appreciate it. "I'm jealous. I've always wanted to learn an instrument. I just never had the knack."

"Persistence." Another light chord. "Plus, when I was little, I could never stay away from it. By the way, mind if we eat in the living room?"

Christie laughed. She was already parking on the couch. "This is where everybody is, right?"

A plate of half-demolished pizza sat on the coffee table in front of Jason. Another plate sat, untouched, to Jason's right, apparently waiting for Rick. That left a space for Christie on Jason's left. She wondered if it was by foresight or by chance that he'd put Jason in the middle. Either way, she decided, definitely a good move.

As she sat down and started to set her plate on the coffee table, Rick scooped a large, squatty glass bowl off the table. "Sorry. You probably don't want turtles on the dinner table."

"Turtles?" Christie straightened and peered into the bowl before Rick could spirit it away. Sure enough, two small green turtles ambled over the rocks resting half-in, half-out of shallow water. "I didn't think you could get those any more."

"Shh. The state of California says no, but some swap meet vendors aren't so fussy." Rick set the bowl on an end table, then took another glance inside it. "Jason," he said impatiently. "There are only two in here again."

Christie had been about to sit back down. Her knees snapped straight. She looked on the couch cushions behind her, then on the floor near her feet, before both

Rick and Jason burst out laughing at her. She looked from one to the other, realizing she'd been had.

"There only *are* two!" Jason giggled at her.

His giggle was too infectious; Christie couldn't glare at him. Instead, she aimed her glare at Rick, but the teasing light in his eyes was just as hard to resist. They'd caught her in that quintessentially female fear of crawly things.

"I was just afraid I'd crush one," she said lamely.

After they'd eaten, Rick let Christie take over the popcorn preparation in the kitchen. He started to load their plates into the dishwasher, then thought better of it. He wasn't sure how many dirty dishes were already inside, or how long they'd been there. They might have gotten pretty disgusting by now.

Christie started the microwave while Jason watched her expectantly. "How often do you guys do this?" she asked.

"Once or twice a year." Rick tried for a simplified version of the family situation. "His mom comes out from Las Vegas to see her sister, and I borrow Jason for a night while they go shopping, or see a movie." He saw the curiosity in Christie's face, and appreciated the way she restrained it. Some details were best not discussed in front of six-year-old boys.

"I'm off school 'til after Christmas," Jason said.

"That's a nice long break," Christie said.

"It's a year-round school," Jason said, making another one of his faces. The faces had been coming fast and furious tonight, all in an effort to impress Christie. Rick knew a crush when he saw one.

He couldn't blame Jason. As Christie poured the popcorn into the oversized bowl on the counter, he watched the way the fluorescent light hit the crown of her head, adding a soft halo of warm red highlights to her hair. Rick took a deep breath. The situation was about as G-rated as it could get. But she'd fit so readily into the homey routine, it felt dangerously cozy.

She raised her head, and Rick gave himself a mental shake. If she had STATION PROPERTY emblazoned across the front of her yellow sweater, it would help. "Now," she said, holding the bag of M&Ms over the bowl. "With or without M&Ms?"

Jason jumped up and down. "M&Ms! M&Ms!"

Rick heaved an elaborate sigh. "I know when I'm licked."

Christie poured a generous layer of M&Ms over the popcorn, and Rick leaned over to look at the colorful candies resting on top of the hot, buttery popcorn. The outer shells made a crackling sound from the heat. "That, Miss Becker," he said, "is sin in a bowl."

She smiled tantalizingly. "Wait'll you taste it," she said, grabbing the bowl and heading back into the living room. And what two healthy, red-blooded males wouldn't follow a beautiful redhead with an armload of candy-covered popcorn?

An hour and a half later, Rick eased himself out from under a limp Jason, whose head had dropped onto his shoulder. Christie stood up to make room as Rick slid the boy's head onto one of the throw pillows on the couch, then stretched his legs out into a semi-comfortable position. Jason never stirred. Even *The Blob* hadn't been enough to keep him awake.

"Kids sleep so hard," she said. "Does he usually make it all the way through the movie?"

"About two-thirds of the time. It's harder Friday nights, when I'm on the air. We get a later start. When he comes over on a Saturday, sometimes we even get two movies in." Rick picked up the throw blanket that hung over the back of the couch and draped it over Jason.

In the moment of quiet that followed, Christie became acutely aware that they'd just lost their chaperone. Time to get out of there fast.

But it would be rude to leave without helping Rick gather the empty glasses from the coffee table. Christie picked up her glass along with the big popcorn bowl, now empty except for a few kernels rattling at the bottom. "All the M&Ms are gone," she pointed out.

"Jason made sure of that. But I got my share, too." Rick led the way into the kitchen. The jeans, Christie noticed again, were a nice change from his usual semicasual dress slacks. They made his long, slim legs that much longer and slimmer.

Forget it. "How long is Jason here with you?"

"Just overnight. Sylvia and his mother pick him up tomorrow after lunch."

Finally, a chance to solve her mental game of who's who. "So Sylvia is—"

"Jason's mom's sister. My ex." Rick finished depositing the dishes into the sink, then leaned back against the dishwasher. Why the dishes hadn't just gone in there, Christie wasn't sure, but she wasn't go-

ing to argue. Besides, she was more interested in the
direction the conversation was taking.

"You two must be on pretty decent terms," she said.
"I guess when I think of divorce, I picture people yell-
ing and throwing plates at each other."

He smiled ruefully. "No, I didn't throw any plates,"
he said. "Can I get you another coke? Or I've got some
instant hot chocolate."

Now was her cue to make a graceful exit. Instead,
she said, "Hot chocolate sounds great." She wasn't
sure if Rick was going to get back to the subject, but
her curiosity was piqued. And it was only ten-thirty,
after all.

Rick walked up, reached for her, and before Christie
could choose between panic and pleasure, he nudged
her gently aside to open the cabinet behind her head.
"Excuse me," he said belatedly, smiling down at her.
Had he noticed her reaction? The touch had been
completely innocent, yet Christie had to wait for the
universe to right itself again.

"It all happened about five years ago." Rick reached
up for a box of cocoa mix. She'd forgotten what they
were talking about. "I was working seven to midnight—you know, at the L.A. station." He glanced at
her, and she nodded. "When you've been married less
than two years, that's not a great schedule." He moved
to another cabinet to retrieve two mugs. "She had an
affair, and she left."

Christie frowned. "*I* would have been throwing
plates."

He surprised her with a grin. "I didn't say it didn't
cross my mind." He mixed the cocoa and water. "It

was ugly for a while. But nothing's all black and white. She worked days, I worked nights, and there were the weekend remotes—" He shrugged. "It wasn't what she expected." He put the two mugs into the microwave. "Plus, the guy she was seeing dumped her in a few weeks. I admit I got a little petty satisfaction out of that." He turned to face her, and Christie had the feeling he wouldn't have told the story if he hadn't had something to do with his hands. "Sorry," he said. "Not a very nice story. But you keep bumping into it by accident, so I thought I might as well get it out of the way."

He was giving her credit for being a lot less nosy than she really was. Tentatively, she ventured, "I'm surprised you're friends now."

"Oh, I wouldn't call it that."

Christie tried to imagine what it had been like. He'd been divorced; she'd never even been to her high school prom. But if her love life had been dull, she realized, she'd also come through it relatively un-scathed. A few dates that hadn't really gotten off the ground, and couple of relationships that had simply ended when the time was right. When she was ready.

She'd never really been hurt. For all her agonizing about being overlooked, she'd never had her heart handed to her in a sling. She decided she didn't envy Rick.

The microwave pinged. Rick took out the mugs and motioned her to the small, round kitchen table.

Christie tried to take a sip from her cup. *Too hot.* "Where does Jason figure in?"

"Oh, right. That's how we got started on this, isn't

it?" Rick managed a sip of the steaming drink with no discernible effort. "He's part of what got us back on civil terms. Sylvia's sister started her divorce right about the time we were finishing ours. The same story, only the shoe was on the other foot—Cindy's husband cheated on her. Seeing the other side of things made Sylvia a little more . . . reasonable. Jason was just a toddler, but he and I were close, even back then. So I helped out by baby-sitting, and got him out of the fray a little bit."

"It's nice of you to keep that relationship going."

"He's a good kid. I think I enjoy it as much as he does." Christie remembered her earlier judgment of Rick, in the station lobby, and felt guilty all over again. "But his mom moved to Las Vegas a couple of years ago, so I don't see him as much any more. It's a good thing Sylvia and I never had children."

The tag ending surprised her. Just when she thought she was getting Rick figured out. She raised her eyebrows. "You didn't want children?"

"Not what I said. But the way things ended up, it would have been a nightmare. Coordinating visits all the time, with someone you used to be married to— even setting things up with Sylvia once or twice a year, there's friction once in a while. And I've seen what Jason got stuck in the middle of." His eyes drifted toward the living room, where the little boy was piled on the couch. "At one point, I would have loved to have kids. But it's not too likely now."

He was surprising her again. Was there something stronger in this cocoa, or what? Christie tried another cautious sip and managed not to burn her tongue.

"You don't think you'll ever remarry?" Hot chocolate nearly sloshed over the top of her mug as she set it down. Rick didn't seem to notice.

"I'm not a good candidate. A workaholic with a raging ego."

"You have a raging ego?"

"Absolutely."

All Christie could think of was how quickly Rick had made room for her on his show. All the punch lines he'd yielded to her, with most of the jokes at his expense. "Do you really believe that, or is that what someone told you?"

Rick's eyes clouded, and for once, Christie was afraid she'd gotten too personal. "Take a guess," he said. He took another drink, and the stormy look passed. "Still, that doesn't mean it isn't true. I work in radio, remember? Raging ego is part of the job description."

"So I have a raging ego, too?"

"Of course." A playful light flickered into Rick's eyes. "Why else in the world would you spend six hours a night alone in a studio? And chuck a decent paying job to do it?"

She shifted uncomfortably. "I don't call that ego." What did she call it? Overcompensating for a mousy adolescence?

He leaned back in his chair, eyeing her triumphantly. "Rampant, raging ego. You're just sneakier about it than most of us. But I know. Under that demure facade, there's a screaming, stomping diva."

Was he flirting with her? She tried her hot chocolate

again. At last, it had reached a comfortable temperature.

Rick switched gears. "So, what would you be doing tonight if you weren't watching an ancient monster movie?"

She chuckled. "Probably watching something every bit as old. Cary Grant, or Jimmy Stewart."

"What is it with you and the past? Everything you like was before you were born."

"Before my *parents* were born," she amended. "Want to hear a dumb story?"

"Sure."

"It all started with a song on the radio."

Rick laughed. "It figures."

She looked down at her cup. "I wasn't the most sociable kid," she confessed. "I spent a lot of time in my bedroom, until I was about sixteen. My big hobby was taping songs off the radio. When I got tired of one station, I'd find another one, until I burned out on all their songs, too. So one day I ran across that old song, 'Key Largo.' You know, the one with all the lyrics about Bogie and Bacall."

"Sure." He was watching her with a bemused smile. "We put it on the play list at the station every once in a while."

"I guess I just got curious. Remember, this is a sixteen-year-old girl with no life." She laughed self-consciously. "So I tracked down the movie, and I loved it. Then someone told me the lyrics had more to do with *Casablanca,* so I watched that, and that was even better. Best movie ever made."

"No," Rick said, "the best movie ever made is *The Godfather.*"

She raised her chin. "You just say that because you're a man. Anyway, after that, I was chasing down Humphrey Bogart movies. Then I started watching the classic movie channels. You were dead on when you teased me about the happy sailor movies. When I heard the old forties music, I was floored. See, one thing kept leading to another. I guess I found out that the more different things you like, the more there is to—" she shrugged, "—like."

He was still smiling. He probably thought she was ridiculous. "That still doesn't explain the country music."

"That, I got from my dad."

There was a brief silence. Rick's smile disappeared. "When did he die?"

She hadn't expected the question. She looked down at her cup again, examining the progressive rings of froth leading down the sides. "How did you know?"

"I picked it up."

She swirled the cup in front of her. "My freshman year in college. Right before Christmas. I figure I was right in the middle of a final when he had a heart attack. No warning." She glanced up at Rick, but the gray eyes were too direct. She had to look back down. "The thing is, I didn't really know him. I was busy being a teenager with the bedroom door closed. And then I went to college. I always think if I'd had a couple more years. . . ."

"So that's why the car." She peeked up again. This time he was smiling, gently. "Don't get me wrong, it's the perfect DJ-mobile. But I couldn't figure out why a loan processor didn't have something newer." He put his hand on the table, letting it rest an inch from hers. "Look, whatever you and your dad didn't say, the car says volumes."

"I know. That's why I keep it running. But even Toyotas don't last forever." She bit her lip.

"So, yours could be the first." His hand inched closer, to squeeze hers. Then he let go, as if any further contact could make them both burst into flames.

No flames at the moment. But his hand did leave behind a feeling of warmth. Christie lifted her own hand from the table.

"Where's your mother now?" he asked.

"She moved to Colorado. We've got lots of family there." She was starting to sound like an abandoned orphan, and that wasn't what she wanted. She shifted the subject back to Rick. "How about your family? Still intact?"

"All alive and well in northern California. I kind of worked my way south. Although they've never understood about the radio thing. My brother still says I was seduced by the dark side."

"What does he do?"

"Investment banker."

Christie acted out a shudder. "I've seen enough three-piece suits to last me the rest of my life."

"He's not so bad. Plus, it's hard to take anyone too seriously when they used to pour sand in your hair."

From that point on, things were back to normal. They talked for another half hour before Christie stood to go.

Reflexively, Rick stood, too. "I'll walk you out."

He probably should have let her go out alone, he thought, but his ingrained manners wouldn't let him. At least that was what he told himself. All he knew was that it was harder than ever to keep his hands to himself; it seemed only natural to reach for her as they walked through the cool California night. Getting out of his apartment should have helped. Instead, it brought back memories of the whole high school dating thing, and all those hesitant front-porch kisses.

But no one was kissing anyone tonight. She was his employee, and he wasn't an idiot.

"Thanks," she said as they reached her car. "It was a nice night."

"Thanks for the M&Ms. You were right. I'm hooked." He assessed her parking spot. The nearest street light was just enough to illuminate the hood of the old Toyota. "I told you to park under a light."

"That was at the station. What is it with you and the chivalry thing, anyway?"

"Just the way I was brought up." Although certain women brought it out more than others. He felt the need to say something more, or maybe he just didn't want her to go. He thought of something he'd been wanting to say for some time. "Christie, I know I gave you a hard time at first. I'm sorry for . . ." He trailed off.

"For what?" she said lightly. "Trying to crush my spirit?"

He laughed. "I don't think that's possible."

"So why'd you do it?" It was hard to make out her expression in the shadows.

Oh, come on. Was she fishing, or did she really have no clue? If she'd parked closer to a bloody street light, the way she should, maybe he'd be able to read her face. "Do you really need to ask me that?" he said quietly.

She was standing just a step away. If she dared to ask, Rick wasn't sure whether she'd be getting her answer in words or not.

Christie's eyes fixed on his for what felt like a long time. Then she took a step back.

"Never mind," she said.

Good. At least one of them had some sense.

She got into her car quickly, before he could help her with the door, which was just as well. Too many more opportunities to touch. Rick watched her taillights fade away. He tried to shut out visions of an alternate reality where both of them were stupid enough to forget who they were, and try out that kiss.

He returned to the front door, started to open it, and growled under his breath. Then, reluctantly, he started ringing the bell to wake Jason up.

He'd locked himself out of his apartment.

Chapter Seven

"Go ahead," Yvonne said. "It's only once a year."

Christie eyed the cranberry red dress on its hanger at the clothing shop. Then she looked at the price tag, and cringed. "Not that one."

"Come on, it's a splurge. Don't you know what this party is really for? Every Christmas the owner of the station flies into town so we can have a party, which gives us an excuse to buy a new dress. It's tradition."

Christie shook her head, and Yvonne looked at her with dawning sympathy. She must have remembered that Christie was on an overnight disc jockey's salary.

"Come over here," Yvonne said, taking her arm. "I just remembered where we should *both* be looking."

At the back of the store was a single, round clearance rack. Christie started to flip her way through the mixture of styles and sizes without much hope. And then she saw it. It was dark green velvet, with skinny little shoulder straps.

"That's a perfect color for you," Yvonne said from over her shoulder.

"And it's a Christmas color. Evergreen." She held her breath and fumbled in the lining for the size. It was right. Then she found the markdown price tag, and she gasped. "Twelve-fifty?" she whispered, afraid a salesperson would hear her and realize the mistake.

"Slow down." Yvonne adopted Christie's hushed tones. "There must be a catch."

They searched until they found it: About one foot of the hem was unstitched. Christie was no seamstress, but even she could fix that. She hurried to the dressing room to try it on before anyone at the store could come to their senses.

When she stepped out a few minutes later, Yvonne said, "Oh, Christie, that's *you.*"

Christie looked in the mirror with some surprise. Her hair had just recently grown to shoulder length; its deep auburn shade made the perfect contrast to the rich green fabric. The dress' simple style made the most of her slim figure. It looked right and it felt right. She tried to reconcile the image in front of her with the skinny, mousy teenager she'd been just a few years ago. Something had happened, and she wasn't sure what or when.

Christie knew she wanted to look good for all the wrong reasons. Rick would be there, but so what? If she got involved with him—assuming he wanted to get involved with her—she could kiss her job good-bye. Still, being around him had a way of making her forget that. Going back to her regular overnight shift this week may have been a comedown, but it had been just in the nick of time.

"See?" Yvonne was saying. "With that dress, a little more makeup, and some spangly earrings . . ."

She'd be all dressed up, with no one to dress up for.

The party was being held at the Santa Moreno Inn. It was an old Spanish mission, renovated into a hotel with banquet facilities. A little shopping district had grown up around it. It was a well-known local landmark, but Christie had never been inside before.

She walked through the inn's courtyard, with moss-grown stone walls and large cherubs looking down at her from archways above. Christmas lights were strung everywhere, most of them white. Christie slowed to admire them, appreciating the holiday feel. She had Christmas decorations up all over her apartment, although she still needed to get a tree.

Cocktails at six, dinner at eight, the memo had said. She walked into the banquet room just after six-thirty and immediately decided she'd arrived too early. The room was still sparsely populated, with about fifteen people milling around the half-dozen or so tables. She didn't spot anyone she knew, and no one had sat down yet. Christie felt like a ship without an anchor. She certainly didn't need an hour and a half for cocktails.

A waiter stopped in front of her with a tray of wine glasses and waited expectantly. She picked one up, and he moved on.

She sidled toward the long banquet table laid out with appetizers, and tried to decide who all these people were. Advertising sales reps, mostly, she guessed, and probably some office staff as well. She didn't spend much time on that side of the building, and the reps were usually out on sales calls. Christie picked up a tiny plate and started debating between the different colors of cheese squares.

"Welcome to the party," said a voice to her left. She looked up to see Ed Arboghast beaming brightly at her. "How's the job going?"

It was the closest she'd been to him since the day she'd first interviewed there. She glimpsed him sometimes in the hallway, going to or from his office, but she still wasn't sure what he did there. She wondered if he'd picked up more weight, lost more hair, or if her memory had simply failed her.

"It's great," she said. *Best pay cut I ever took,* she thought, but decided it wouldn't sound right.

Mr. Arboghast introduced her to his wife, a pleasant middle-aged woman, while Christie politely sipped her wine. She didn't care much for wine and liked red even less, but it gave her something to do with her hands.

"Try the shrimp," Mr. Arboghast smiled. "It's really good." And he tottered off.

More people had arrived, and the noise level in the room was starting to come up. Christie was turning back toward the table, in search of the recommended shrimp, when Rick walked in.

It wasn't just the way he looked in a coat and tie, so soon after Christie had said she'd seen enough suits to last a lifetime. It wasn't just the way the rich gray of the suit matched the color of his eyes, or the care he'd taken tonight to replace his hair's usual appealing, tousled look with an appealing, smooth look.

It was the look in his eyes when he saw her, from twenty feet away, that floored her. He'd picked her out instantly, just a few steps into the room. His first, undisguised reaction told her plainly that he liked what he saw. To compound the effect, he didn't look away, and Christie felt a dangerous spark somewhere in the vicinity of her heart.

All the song lyrics she'd ever heard about eyes meeting across a crowded room stopped being clichés. She had to catch her breath. And she had to do it quickly, because now he was walking straight toward her.

Only to be intercepted by Mr. Arboghast, who led him to a silver-haired, black-suited man she'd never seen before. The station's owner, no doubt.

Christie looked away, feeling like a deer rescued from the headlights of an approaching car. Suddenly, she could move again. She took another sip from her glass and instantly felt sorry she had. A warm, queasy feeling took hold, and all at once the room felt very loud and very crowded.

She looked down at her glass. The wine was nearly half gone. Idiot. She hadn't had anything to eat since lunch, and she'd never gotten hold of any of the appetizers. Her queasiness grew. Christie set the glass down on the banquet table and quickly headed outside for some air.

She stepped into the courtyard and was hit by the shock of the cool, damp night around her. Christie inhaled deeply and found it did wonders. The fresh, earthy scent reminded her of a recent rain, but it was probably just the moisture from the abundance of plants out here.

The quiet was refreshing, too. Christie wandered down a walkway that led away from the main hotel complex, toward a wooden bridge over a small pond. Across the bridge, the walkway continued toward the shops. Christie stopped on the bridge and leaned her arms on the waist-high rail to look down into the water. Much better, if a little chillier. She'd checked her coat when she arrived in the banquet room; she rubbed her bare arms against the light breeze.

Her brief wooziness cleared, and her thoughts went back to what was waiting for her inside the banquet room. She had to be careful. That look from Rick had thrown her off balance, and she couldn't afford to make a fool of herself tonight. Anything beyond friendship was out of the question, and he knew that as well as she did. She'd probably imagined that look on his face, or misread it. He'd probably been coming over to tell her that her slip was showing or something.

She looked down at the dress. What a waste. She'd spent an unusual amount of time—for her—getting ready tonight, fussing with her hair and makeup. She'd tried to tell herself she wanted to make a good impression on everyone, certainly not Rick in particular, but she knew better.

And for what? To remind herself she shouldn't be thinking about Rick at all.

A footstep on the bridge interrupted her thoughts. "Christie?"

No point in pretending she didn't know *that* voice.

Christie looked up without surprise, as if she'd expected Rick to show up all along. She'd have to have a talk with the back of her mind about these little fantasies. They seemed to have a way of coming true.

"Are you all right?" he said as he reached her. "You looked a little green when you walked out."

He'd been flanked by two executive types. How could he have possibly seen her walk out? Yet, obviously he had.

"I'm okay. I just needed some air. The wine hit me all of a sudden."

He frowned. "That doesn't sound like you."

"It's not. I had half a glass. It hit my stomach, not my head." She laughed. "I'm not very used to it."

"Plus the fact that you weigh about five pounds." He leaned sideways against the rail, studying her. Always that relaxed posture, always those watching eyes. "Sure you're okay?"

"Fine. It's nice out here."

Rick nodded. "Very nice." He glanced at his watch. "Want to walk for a little bit? I've already schmoozed the boss and the owner."

It sounded harmless enough, or so she told herself. It also sounded a lot more appealing than going back inside to mingle. "Sure."

Rick pointed them down the other side of the bridge, away from the hotel. She said, "I'm surprised none of the other jocks are here yet."

"Yvonne got here a minute ago. Rob's probably picking up his date."

"He's bringing a date?"

"I think so. He's the only one who ever does."

It hadn't occurred to Christie before that none of the disc jockeys were married. Of course, Rick had been, once. She decided to leave that subject alone tonight.

They passed under a lattice woven with climbing plants. "This is a beautiful place." Hadn't she said that already? "They really went all out."

"Trade," Rick said.

"What?"

"Station trade. That's how they paid for this party. You'll be hearing a slew of commercials soon. It's a lot cheaper than real money."

"Cynic."

"Just the truth. I cut the commercial myself this afternoon."

"That's no reason not to enjoy it."

"I didn't say I wasn't enjoying it." His eyes were on her again. There was a warm note in his voice, and Christie felt it like a physical touch. She realized she'd unintentionally been walking closer to Rick, as if the space between them didn't belong there. She widened the distance, and reached up to snap one of the little pink flowers from the latticework overhead. "Look," she said. "Bougainvillea."

"Gesundheit."

They reached the cobblestone block of shops. Christie was about to suggest turning around, but a window display of Christmas decorations caught her eye, and she hurried forward. One Victorian angel with a trumpet reminded her of the tree-topper her mother used to put on the tree all the years Christie was growing up.

She'd given it to Christie before she moved away to Colorado.

"Have you decorated your place yet?" she asked when Rick caught up to her.

"A little."

She looked at him suspiciously. "You're not one of those Scrooges, are you? I'd be playing a lot more Christmas music on the station by now if I were you."

"Some people complain if we do."

" 'Some people' isn't everybody," she said. She couldn't imagine the holidays without Christmas music. "What about you?"

"Nothing against Christmas," he said. "It just doesn't have the best associations for me."

She was starting to recognize that tone of voice. It was the one he used whenever his divorce came up. Christie looked up in time to see his eyes darken under the street light. "I walked into it again, didn't I?"

"With both feet."

The woman left him at *Christmas?* "I'm sorry," she said again.

"It's okay." His eyes went back to the window. "Any particular songs you want me to add?"

"For Christmas?" She looked up in surprise. "What, you're taking requests?"

"It's a one-night offer."

"Well, any of the old carols. And 'White Christmas,' by Bing Crosby."

"You *would* use Christmas for an excuse to make me play Bing Crosby."

They walked on in companionable silence. The shops were closed, so they had the area almost to themselves. The loudest sound came from Christie's heels on the cobblestones. Her new height brought Rick a little closer to eye level. She caught herself veering toward him again, and veered away, rubbing her arms again. The breeze was getting stronger, and nippier.

"Cold?"

"A little."

"Why do women wear dresses without sleeves this time of year?"

"Why do men wear heavy suits in the summer?"

"Women make us."

A fresh breeze blasted hard enough to send the remaining fall leaves skittering around them. Christie shivered. Rick pulled her toward the doorway of one of the shops, where a window display jutted outward, providing a shelter from the wind. "Here." He slipped his jacket off and draped it over her shoulders. "You wear the suit for a change."

The jacket was warm from being on him. It smelled like Rick, too, a scent she recognized without being able to define it. He studied her for a moment with a look of mock appraisal, and Christie felt more dizzy than she had half an hour ago from the wine.

He took the bougainvillea blossom from her hand and tucked it into the button of the jacket's lapel. "There," he smiled. "Perfect."

He patted down her shoulders, and slowly the smile faded.

In his eyes was a replay of the look from across the room, only this time at much closer range. Even the crickets seemed to get quieter. Then Rick muttered something under his breath that Christie couldn't quite make out, and brought his mouth down to hers.

It never occurred to her to stop him.

First kisses weren't supposed to be like this. There was no fumbling, no hesitation, just an immediate connection, as if he'd thought about this for a long time. It was gentle at first, but not quite tentative, building slowly as she responded. And it was thorough. She hadn't believed a kiss could literally make you weak in the knees, until now. The only problem was that it ended.

He raised his head, but his hands stayed on her shoulders. "I shouldn't have done that." His mouth was still close to hers.

"No," she agreed, not moving. "It was a terrible idea." She put her arms around his neck, and he moved forward, closing the rest of the space between them. His mouth covered hers again.

She knew this couldn't go anywhere. She knew there was no point. But she'd already thrown reason out the window. All she could think of was making the moment go on as long as she could. What was it her mother said? Might as well be hanged for stealing a sheep as a lamb? Whatever it was, she wasn't acting on mother's advice right now. If this was temporary insanity, she wanted it to last.

"This is crazy," Rick whispered, echoing her jumbled thoughts. Then he kissed her again, and she stopped thinking at all.

She leaned back against the door frame behind her, drinking in the warmth of his closeness. Slowly, his hands left her shoulders, one going up to wind his fingers through her hair. The other slipped under the jacket to circle her waist. Christie couldn't believe she'd been cold a few minutes ago.

He finally raised his lips from hers, and for a moment she was afraid he was going to let go. Instead, he bent his head down to the side of her throat. "I knew you'd be trouble," he murmured. There was a huskiness in his voice that she'd never heard before. His lips brushed over her skin, and a tiny moan escaped from the back of her throat. She felt Rick's arm tighten around the small of her back. Christie sighed. This temporary insanity thing would have to—

Suddenly Rick froze and took two steps back, as if she were a live coal. A moment later Christie understood why. Footsteps. The muffled sound on the cobblestones was like a burglar alarm.

What had they been thinking? Work wasn't miles away; it was yards away.

She stood upright from the door where she'd been leaning, and Rick's jacket fell to the ground. They both dove for it. Christie got it first, handed it to Rick, then spun around to look into the shop window they'd been oblivious to just moments before. Behind her, she could hear Rick hastily shrugging his jacket back on.

The window held a display of expensive-looking antique furniture. "I love the Victrola," she said, amazed at the normalcy in her voice.

"Probably a reproduction," Mr. Arboghast's voice said behind them.

Whew. It didn't get any closer than that. Christie turned, and there the boss stood with his wife. Both of them were smiling benignly. No sign that either one had seen anything amiss. "What are you kids doing out here?" Mr. Arboghast said.

"Window shopping," she said.

"You picked out a great place, Ed," Rick said. "It sure beats the Ramada Inn last year."

"Oh, Francis gets the credit for that." Mr. Arboghast patted his wife's hand, tucked through his arm.

"I told him about it," she explained. "I was here for a luncheon this summer."

As the small talk went on, Christie had time to calm down and start mentally kicking herself for her stupidity. Finally Mr. Arboghast walked away, his wife on his arm.

"It's windy out here, Rick," he called back over his shoulder. "You should give the lady your jacket."

Chapter Eight

Christie stood next to him, staring into the shop window until the boss was out of earshot. Rick had to hand it to her for a quick recovery. After that embrace, he'd forgotten the store was there. Even now, he didn't think his heart rate was back to normal. Whether that was from kissing Christie, or from the close call afterward, he wasn't sure.

When Ed was safely out of earshot, Christie said, "I imagine it would look better if we went back in separately." She turned around without so much as looking at him, and headed back toward the banquet room.

"Christie, wait." Rick fell into step beside her. Those high heels were making remarkably good time for someone who was trying to be so casual. Why was she in such a hurry now? They hadn't gotten caught, and it was a little late to cover up. "Christie, it's not like we killed someone."

"Isn't it?" She kept walking, eyes straight ahead.

Whoa. Time for a little perspective here. "Listen to yourself for a second. And slow down." They were covering the cobblestone sidewalk much faster than they had coming the other direction, and they both needed to get a grip before they went back into that room.

"Don't you see, Rick?" She was trying to sound conversational, as if they were talking about the weather. In case someone was eavesdropping behind the shrubbery? "What would have happened if he'd gotten there a little sooner?"

He honestly wasn't sure. "Well, it wouldn't have been good. But I don't think we would have been sent to the gallows. Maybe a written reprimand?"

"The first thing in my personnel file after my W-2 form."

Ten minutes after kissing him until his legs nearly quit, all she could think about was her own neck. The trouble was, he was thinking about her neck, too, and the way her perfume had smelled. If their embrace had just come from the heat of the moment, it was taking a long time to fade.

But he could be as practical and cold-blooded as she was. "Now, hold on," he said. "You're not the only one with something at stake here."

"No. But who's going to come off worse?" Christie stopped and turned so suddenly he almost stepped on her foot. The look on her face was one of desperate, unadulterated panic. "You've been with the company what, five years? And you're a man. I'm a woman who came out of nowhere a couple of months ago. Some professional. They'd never take me seriously again."

The words had a certain logic to them. "You've thought about this." *When?* he wondered. Ten minutes ago, he'd been doing anything but thinking.

She started walking again. "I can't believe I was so stupid."

Now, *that* was a little insulting. But she'd made her point. It would look worse for her, and she couldn't afford that. If that wasn't enough to make him stick to company rules and keep his hands to himself, nothing was.

They crossed over the little wooden bridge, where things had begun so innocently half an hour before. Just a little moonlight stroll between friends. *Yeah, right.* As if he couldn't have seen this coming. She was right. It had been a mistake. A big, fat mistake, and the sooner they put it behind them, the better.

They walked the rest of the way to the banquet room in silence. Before he opened the door, his ego still smarting, Rick couldn't resist one parting shot. "Christie?"

"What?"

"If you're concerned about the way things look, you might want to fix your lipstick."

Momentarily pleased by her horrified look, he went inside ahead of her.

It had been a snappy line, but Rick had plenty of time to regret it in the next two hours. Sometimes a clever quip wasn't worth the trouble it caused.

Both of them sat at the table where the rest of the

jocks had already settled in. Anything else would have looked out of place. Rick watched as Christie sandwiched herself next to Yvonne, apparently trying to sit as far away from him as possible. She wound up straight across from him, and he was sure that wasn't what she'd had in mind. Instead of avoiding him, she was in a spot where the opportunities for eye contact were endless.

It was quite a view, actually. Christie's troubled expression wasn't enough to detract from the way she looked in that green dress. It brought out the green in her hazel eyes, which looked achingly soulful whenever they met his by accident. So she did have a heart. His annoyance faded. Before guilt could take over, Rick replaced it with self-justification. All right, so he'd started it. He just hadn't expected her to transform herself into a siren for the night. Maybe that was why he'd lost his head. Easy enough to blame it on the dress.

Except that Yvonne, on Christie's right, was wearing a black dress every bit as stunning. And Rob's date, on her left, was wearing something so silver and sequinny it was practically blinding. The one Rick couldn't stop looking at—try as he might—was the redhead in the middle. She may have recovered more quickly under the eyes of the general manager, but now she looked sicker than she had when she left the room earlier.

But if it was keeping up appearances she cared about, he was giving her that in spades. He chatted and laughed his way through dinner, barely aware of what he was saying. Detachment. It was an old survival mechanism. It was how you got through an air shift the night after your wife left you. It was how you avoided getting seriously involved with anyone in all the years after that. Until the one woman you had absolutely no business getting involved with came along and—

"My first live broadcast," he said, "was for this little station in Lancaster. A Fourth of July fireworks display. And the entertainment before the fireworks—I swear I'm not making this up—was an eight-year-old boy in a gold lame Elvis suit . . ."

He wasn't the only one looking at Christie. Rob was doing it too, although Rob's eyes always got around, date or no date.

". . .the kid's lip-synching to songs on a CD boom box . . ."

Rick threw another quick glance at Christie. She didn't seem to notice Rob's stare, but she wasn't looking at Rick, either. Or eating her chicken.

". . .so of course the power goes out on the boom box . . ."

Out of the blue, Yvonne asked, "Is that a new fashion statement, Rick?"

He looked at her blankly, then glanced down. The little pink blossom, now slightly crushed, was still tucked into the buttonhole of his lapel. Across the table, Christie looked aghast, as if Yvonne had pointed out a bleeding corpse on the floor at Rick's feet.

"Just a souvenir from outside." He shrugged. "They're growing all over the place out there."

But he left it in his lapel for the rest of the night.

MEMO TO: On-Air Staff
FROM: Rick Fox
RE: Holiday schedule

'Tis the season to. . .work like a dog.

Before I make up the schedule for Christmas Eve and Christmas Day, I'm looking for full-timers and part-timers willing to volunteer for some of these hard-to-fill shifts. I'm hoping to fill as many slots as possible on a volunteer basis before I'm forced to do the dirty work of assigning them.

Those who volunteer will be rewarded, not only in the next life, but also with a comp day off. And I promise, I'll remember you when it's time to make up the next holiday schedule.

Thanks in advance. And Merry Christmas.
Rick

Christie wondered if the "Merry Christmas" was meant to be sincere or satirical. She also wondered if she was trying to be a martyr when she signed up for the Christmas Eve shift.

She stepped behind the counter in the on-air studio, ready to trade sides with Rob the way they always did. Tonight it felt different. "We're doing this at the wrong time," she said. Rob had taken the afternoon shift on Christmas Eve day, while Christie had signed up for 6 P.M. to midnight.

Rob looked up at the ceiling. "Too bad there's no mistletoe in here."

"In your dreams." If he only knew the trouble she'd let herself get into, without any mistletoe.

"Oh, well. Merry Christmas." Rob started to move past her as usual, then paused. "You're not sad, are you?"

He wasn't as shallow as he looked. "A little," she said. "Just trying not to feel pathetic."

He really wasn't so bad. In the course of their five-minute nightly encounters, Christie had actually come to like Rob quite a bit. If she'd ever taken him up on one of his lighthearted passes, she still wasn't sure what he'd do, but he never pushed it. It was more of a running joke than anything else.

"I know how you feel," he said. "Sometime it's tough being single at Christmas when you don't have any family in town." He put his jacket on over a bright red sweater.

"You're on your way to a party, aren't you?" she said.

"Yeah, well. No point being miserable alone."

True to his word, Rick had added Bing Crosby's "White Christmas" to the play list, along with a healthy helping of traditional carols. And from 6 P.M. on, Christmas music was all they were playing.

Christie took a few phone calls from people to see how they were spending their Christmas Eve, but the calls were sparse, and most of them were from people who were alone. Those were too depressing to air. She did have some fun doing something she'd always wanted to do: broadcasting updates of Santa sightings in the sky as he made his way toward California from the East Coast. But there was no denying that working on Christmas Eve was a proposition ripe for self-pity.

She hadn't seen Rick since the party. She'd made sure of it. It was easy enough to do, just by sticking to her normal, assigned work schedule. She hadn't seen him, but she'd had endless one-sided conversations with him in her mind. Sometimes she blamed him for everything. Sometimes she admitted to her part in the kiss, but before she knew it, she was admitting to a whole lot more, and they dissolved into another heart-melting clinch. Telling him off was safer, even if it wasn't any more realistic. But no matter what scenario she chose, Christie could never quite imagine what Rick would say, aside from pointing out that they hadn't killed anyone.

No matter what Rick said or didn't say in those imaginary conversations, it didn't matter. The bottom line was still the same. They had to go on as if none of it had happened, because it could never happen again. She'd known that going in. But now, in hindsight, it was a high price to pay for a few minutes.

A few incredible minutes.

A lush version of "Silent Night" ended with a flourish of strings. As the last chord faded, Christie thought she heard the sound effect of sleigh bells. On "Silent Night?" She frowned and started the next song. The jingling persisted. Christie turned down the volume on the monitor speakers.

It was coming from out in the hallway.

Before she could go out to investigate, the studio door opened, and Rick walked in. Christie raised her hands to her face, not quite believing what she was seeing. He was wearing a fuzzy red Santa hat and shaking a two-foot string of Christmas bells. The hat lopped over to one side; his grin was faintly embarrassed. She couldn't help but laugh.

"Special delivery," he said. Rick brought his other hand from behind his back to set a fair-sized gift bag on the countertop between them, next to the guest microphone.

She recovered from laughing and lowered her hands from her face. The one thing she wasn't going to do was fall all over him. But she had to admit, he'd cheered her up.

"Merry Christmas," he said. He reached across the counter and dropped the Santa hat onto her head. "This looks better on you than it does me."

She stared at the bag on the counter, where cartoon reindeer danced on a red and green background. "I didn't get you—"

"And why should you? Here, I'll help you open it. It wouldn't be a good idea to shake this package." He lifted a shallow glass bowl out of the bag and set it on the countertop.

Inside was a turtle, like the ones from Rick's apartment. Christie blinked, quickly. She knew he was going for just the right level of absurdity. She wasn't going to get all gooey about it.

"It's sweet," she said. "Thanks."

"Very low maintenance, too. I thought about saddling you with a twenty-gallon tank of tropical fish, but it was too heavy to carry."

She smiled, but she couldn't look at Rick. Instead, she studied the little green turtle, marching resolutely on a wet rock at the bottom of the bowl with nowhere to go.

"What's his name?" Rick asked her.

Christie hesitated for half a second. "Bing."

"I should have known." She could feel him watching her face.

Just in time, she realized her song was ending. Hurriedly, she cued the next one, grateful for the interruption. She had no idea what to say next.

"Nice job on the Santa reports," Rick said. "Your news training is coming in handy."

"Thanks." That was safe to talk about. "That's why I picked this shift."

"I was betting on either sainthood or masochism. How are you spending your Christmas tomorrow?"

"Turkey dinner at my girlfriend Alicia's. The one who rescued me the morning after my car broke down." That seemed eons ago. "Aren't you going anywhere?" On the posted schedule, he'd put himself down for the Christmas afternoon shift.

"I decided to wait for the weekend. My folks are about five hours north of here. There'll be less traffic, and this way I'm around if anything comes up at the station." And, Rick admitted to himself, it gave him a chance to deliver Christie's present. Now, he braced himself for the hard part. "I haven't seen you around the station lately."

"I had a lot of shopping to do."

"That's fine. No one expects you to put in all the extra time you've been doing. I'd just hate to think anything I did was keeping you away."

Christie looked up at him, and Rick could see her

fighting to keep her expression guarded. She wasn't very good at it. And darn it, she was biting the corner of her lip. Rick tried to stay focused on her eyes.

He'd opened the subject. No going back now. "Christie, about the other night." Rick took a deep breath, leaned his palms on the counter, and prepared to launch into the most elaborate set of half-truths he'd ever come up with.

"Let's just forget about it," she said.

He nodded. "Okay. But first, I owe you an apology. I got carried away, and I imagine I've made things pretty uncomfortable for you." He gripped the counter a little harder, glad it was there between them. In spite of what he was saying, there was nothing he would have liked better than to grab her again and kiss her, right now, and he couldn't let her know that. Ever.

There were times when over ten years of experience performing came in handy.

"Don't worry about it." Christie shrugged. "I guess we both got a little carried away."

She was learning. Already, she was getting better at her nonchalance. Rick was still pretty sure it was an act. But so what if it wasn't? More power to her.

He could have quit while he was ahead. Instead, he took another deep breath and drove a few more nails into his coffin. He had to kill any interest on her side, because he didn't trust himself. "There's an ugly truth about men," he said. "We have a hard time remembering what 'platonic' is." Sure. Blame it all on his male programming. He knew better. "The thing is, you're a valuable employee, and I wouldn't want anything to jeopardize that. I know what this job means to you, and I was way out of line. It won't happen again."

"Fine," Christie's eyes were devoid of expression now. "We're both grown-ups, right?"

"Right." He shouldn't have put the Santa hat on her. The oversized cap hung almost over her eyebrows, giving her a waifish look. She would have hated the idea of being seen as a waif. If she only knew. Rick could picture her under the Christmas tree—his Christmas tree—wearing that hat, wrapped up in a soft robe, waiting to open their gifts. And that could never be.

"So," he said, "can we get back to where we were before?"

"Sure," she said. But Rick knew the damage had been done. He'd done more than start something they couldn't possibly finish, or even mess up a working relationship. He'd lost a friend.

He reached over one more time to tweak her Santa cap. He caught a flash of hurt in her eyes, and knew he had to leave it there. It was for her own good.

"Enough said." Christie made the gesture of turning a key over her lips and tossing it away over her shoulder. An appropriate gesture in more ways than one.

On Christmas morning, Christie opened the presents under the small tree in her living room. Most of them were from her family in Colorado. A few days ago at work, Yvonne had given her a funny little pin with musical notes, decked with glitter and surrounded by feathers. That made two people at work she owed presents to.

She called her mother. Hearing the familiar voice,

always full of love and concern, Christie almost broke down and told her everything. She remembered calling home from summer camp when she was ten years old, crying because some of the other kids had gone swimming without her.

Today, instead, she said "I love you," thanked her mother for the sweater she'd sent, and said everything was fine. Christie knew Mom wasn't buying it, but with true motherly wisdom, she didn't press. She'd always been good about things like that.

Still, the call did her good. By the time Christie hung up the phone, she'd made up her mind: It was time to grow up.

What in the world was she doing, at twenty-six years old, mooning over her boss? It was time to get over Rick Fox and get back to what was important. She didn't have time or energy for any relationship right now, let alone an impossible relationship with someone who could shake her off like someone's homely kid sister. She was heading for a new year. Time to make a new start.

With that decided, she fed Bing, got dressed, put on her makeup and went to Christmas dinner at Alicia's.

"So, are you seeing anyone?"

The question came at a bad time. Rick nearly choked on his apple cider.

He glared across the table at his brother, David. "Not really." He kept his tone casual for the rest of the family's benefit.

It didn't work. David's wife, Carol, leaned forward beside him. "Oh? What does *'really'* mean?"

"It means what it says. Really." This time the irritation showed in his voice. More heads turned his way. Drat. It was nice of them to hold off Christmas dinner until he got there, but he hadn't figured on being the main course. He glanced down at his plate. The dumplings were as good as ever, but he wasn't eating much.

His mother chimed in. "You know, just because things didn't work out with Sylvia doesn't mean—"

"You're right. It doesn't." Rick restored his pleasant tone. It worked with listeners. It had worked with Christie, sort of. It could work with his family, too. He reached for his sparkling cider again. "What's going on here, anyway? After five years I'm fair game?" He nodded at his very pregnant sister-in-law. "Worried about the family line dying out, just because David couldn't produce a boy?" He winked at Carol to let her know the shot wasn't aimed at her.

It didn't work. Carol sat up straighter. "I *wanted* a girl!"

Oh, well. At least he'd changed the subject.

When Rick got back to work two days later, a plate of brownies was waiting on his desk, with a card from Christie. Just her signature. Nothing else. The unwritten note said, *Here's something I owe you.*

Later that afternoon, there was a familiar sound he hadn't heard in a while: the sound of girlish laughter, coming from Yvonne's office across the hall. Christie Becker was back.

And she was ignoring him for all she was worth.

Chapter Nine

There was a rattle of glass and metal as the outside door by the studio was propped open, with a little more noise than necessary. Judging by the clatter, Rob was back from his live remote broadcast. Soon Rob was loudly schlepping the first load of equipment down the hall and back to its storage place in the transmitter room.

Inside Yvonne's office, Christie and Yvonne grinned at each other. "Think Rob's hinting he could use a little help?" Yvonne said.

Christie had helped to load up for a few remotes herself, and most of the equipment wasn't that heavy. "My heart bleeds for him."

"That'll be you in a couple of weeks," Yvonne said.

"What?"

"Your first live broadcast. It's in about two weeks. Didn't Rick tell you?"

Rick hadn't told her much of anything lately, although he'd been a study in casual friendliness for the past few weeks. He never failed to greet her in the hallway, and he always seemed to have some little piece of small talk handy—always pleasant, always brief, and never about anything that mattered. She knew he was going out of his way to show her they could still be friends. Some days she almost expected him to give her a buddy-buddy punch in the arm: *No hard feelings, right? Hey, how about those Dodgers?*

It was so easy for him to pick up as if nothing had ever happened. It didn't say much for her. On bad days, it still hurt. On good days, Christie could work up a healthy case of resentment, and that helped. He'd been the one to take them in a direction they never should have gone. And then, when it was over and he came to his senses, he simply stepped back, shrugged, and moved on. She'd long since concluded that Bing had simply been a pat on the head, a little dose of holiday guilt. It didn't stop her from taking good care of him; she bought him a larger bowl and some bigger, shinier rocks. After all, why blame an innocent turtle?

And whenever Rick greeted her in the hallway, Christie was always careful to respond in kind. She kept her replies bright, cheerful, and short. Remembering her New Year's resolution, she refused to let it drive her crazy. But in its own way, the bland friendliness was worse than the old days when he'd barely spoken to her at all.

Somehow, in the midst of all those little chats about the weather, he'd neglected to mention a major milestone like her first live remote broadcast.

"Are you serious?" she asked Yvonne. She felt a now-familiar knot of excitement, laced with panic.

"I've seen that look before," Yvonne said. "Relax. You know you can do it."

Christie grinned. "It's okay. I finally figured out it's part of the process with me. I have to panic before I try something new. You know, I still have this little moment of terror before I go on the air. I kind of like it. It's like slaying a dragon every night."

Rick chimed in from the doorway. "Have you had "The Dream" yet?"

His appearance in here was a little unusual, but Christie tried not to act surprised. Just another round in the game of playing normal. "The Dream?"

"That's what we call it," Yvonne said. "I think every jock has it sometimes."

Rick had taken his old favorite stance, leaning against the door frame, arms folded. A sheet of paper dangled from one hand. "It's this recurring dream, where you're on the air and the music runs out. Over and over. Sometimes it feels like it goes on for hours."

"Everybody has that?" Christie said. "I started having that back when I was in broadcasting school."

"I had a new version a couple of months ago," Yvonne said. "The Christmas music kept coming on, no matter what I put in the CD player."

"And it *never goes away,*" Rick said ominously. "I've got a friend from the old college station who's been teaching math for nearly ten years, and he still has it." He strolled to the photocopier and loaded the sheet of paper into the machine.

Well, that hadn't been so bad. Probably their longest

conversation since Christmas Eve, and Christie felt almost normal. Maybe she was getting the hang of this just-friends thing.

Then she noticed he was wearing jeans, and frowned. Rick never wore jeans to work. These weren't the same ones she'd seen that night at his apartment, but they made his legs look just as long and lean. *Stop it.* She wasn't supposed to notice things like that. Christie went back to opening a new CD from the afternoon mail, pulling the tab on the brown padded envelope with a long, slow rip.

"Hey, legs," Yvonne said easily. "Been back on the treadmill lately?"

"Not really," Rick said. "Just lost a couple of pounds."

Just like that, any delusions of normalcy went out the window. Sure. Yvonne could flirt with Rick all she wanted. Christie's mind erupted with useless jealousy. She tried to ignore it, but it was like having a blender turned on inside her. Idiotic thoughts whirred through her head and wouldn't shut up. Yvonne knew about the treadmill. Which meant she'd probably been in Rick's apartment, too. He probably made passes at every female who worked for him.

It was crazy, and she knew it. She had to get out of here, at least for a minute. "I'll be back," she said to Yvonne. Christie launched out of her chair and headed down the hall.

The door leading outside still stood propped open, so she went in that direction. The van was parked at the curb, with most of the equipment still inside from

Rob's live broadcast. Christie busied herself getting some of the gear out.

"Christie? What are you doing?"

It was Rick again. Couldn't she ever walk out of a room without him noticing?

"I'm unloading the van," she said, fighting for that bland cheerfulness. She hefted a crate full of extension cords down to the ground behind the van, avoiding Rick's attempt to take it from her hands. She leaned back in to reach for a speaker.

"Christie, you don't have to do this."

"Why not?" She put on a wide smile. "I hear I have a remote coming up in a few weeks. I might as well get the practice, right?"

The speaker was heavy for her, and clumsy. But once again, she avoided his attempt to help her, and set it down.

On his foot.

Rick bellowed, and Christie scrambled to get the speaker off his toes. Rick lifted it first, then crouched to examine his foot. Christie bent down, too, reflexively putting a hand on his shoulder.

"Rick! Are you okay?"

He looked up at her, and she winced at his stone-gray glare. It had been an accident. Didn't he know that? "Rick, I'm sorry."

Their eyes locked, and the glare faded. It was replaced by an expression Christie couldn't identify. Whatever it was, it made her just as uncomfortable. Clouds, she thought. His eyes were like twin gray clouds, and she'd never be able to see what was really behind them. While all her reactions, she was sure, were written all over her face. It wasn't fair. Christie became aware of her hand on his shoulder, and took it away. She straightened up and stepped back.

"It's okay," he said. He made a grimace that looked half-real, half-joking. "Of course, I'll never walk again . . ."

He straightened, reaching out to take her arm for a little leverage. His eyes didn't leave hers. Christie needed to find an excuse to walk away, fast, but her brain felt as paralyzed as the rest of her. For lack of anything else to say, she started to apologize again. "I didn't mean to—"

"Hey, what's all the ruckus?" Rob said, finally returning from his lengthy break.

"Oh, nothing." Rick let go of her arm, but he still didn't look away. He smiled wryly. "Becker was just taking out her frustrations on me."

"Oh." Rob picked up the offending speaker effortlessly. "I thought she only did that with me." He winked at Christie and went back inside.

For absolutely no reason, she felt her face go red.

Rick stared after Rob as he went inside, then turned back to Christie and snapped: "What's that supposed to mean?"

The force of his glare startled her. "It doesn't *mean* anything." Immediately she was sorry she'd denied it. "And what if it did?"

"Oh, nothing." Rick's eyes took on a cool, appraising look. "I just thought you were concerned about your professional reputation."

Weeks of hurt, embarrassment and resentment

boiled over inside her. Christie shot Rick a look that she hoped was as fiery as his was cold.

"Watch out for your other foot," she said, and went back inside.

Great. They'd both just managed to descend from high school down to the sixth grade level.

Christie could still feel the heat in her face as she went back to Yvonne's office. Then she remembered the conversation that had sent her out of the room. She wasn't sure she wanted to be here, either. Across the hall behind her, she heard Rick's door quietly and emphatically shut.

Yvonne turned her head away from her computer screen. She peered across the hall, eyebrows raised. "I've never seen *that* before. What's going on?"

"I dropped a speaker on his foot," Christie said irritably. "He's probably in there licking his wounds, if you want to go in and hold his hand."

"Hey!" Yvonne's eyes flashed. "What was *that* for?"

There had never been a harsh word between the two of them before. This day had turned into a total nightmare, all in less than fifteen minutes. Christie pressed a hand to her forehead and clenched the bangs of her hair. "Yvonne, I'm sorry. Whatever you do with Rick is your business. I just—"

"What?" Yvonne spun her chair completely around to face her. "Christie, what the heck are you talking about?"

The surprise on Yvonne's face looked utterly genuine. Christie felt more foolish than ever. She dropped her hand to her side, and they stared at each other for several long, slow beats.

Yvonne whispered, "You've got a crush on Rick!" Her look of dawning comprehension turned into something like glee. "Honey, that's—"

The glee faded into horror. "Oh, honey, that's awful."

In a flash, Yvonne reached into her desk drawer and grabbed her purse. "Let's go. You and I have got to talk."

Rick stared at the closed door of his office. It made the room feel smaller, and somehow dimmer. He could even imagine there was less air to breathe.

Leaning back in his chair, he put his feet up on the desk and eyed the fresh scuff mark on his right loafer. The damage went a lot further than a scuffed shoe and a sore toe. Just friends. Who was he kidding?

He had no idea what had sent Christie barreling out of the office to haul speakers. But he knew perfectly well why he'd acted like a jerk, and it was ridiculous. Jealous of a comment from Rob? Rob would flirt with anything that walked. It had nearly cost him his job, a couple of times over. Christie was too smart to fall for anything like that.

On the other hand, she might be emotionally vulnerable lately. Rick had himself to thank for that. And she saw Rob alone in the studio. Every night.

Maybe, just to be safe, he should have a little talk with Rob about not hitting on impressionable newcomers.

Or maybe not.

Rick knew his judgment was getting cloudy, and he didn't like it. There was no point in any of this, not with both of their jobs on the line. The job fit her like skin, and he had no business asking her to risk it, or to give it up. It was one of the things he loved about her.

Love. He hadn't meant to think that. It was just there, as natural as breathing.

And it was impossible. He'd just have to stop breathing.

Love. Based on what? A couple of lovely evenings, one great week in the studio, and one kiss.

Well, all right. One really amazing series of kisses.

It had felt more than good. It had felt *right.* The same way it felt right to have her there in his apartment, making popcorn as though she'd done it countless times before.

But it wasn't right. It couldn't be. Not when Christie worked for him. Not when the owner of the business—not the most flexible man, from what Rick had seen—had a hard-and-fast policy against managers getting involved with employees. There was no way around it.

And there was no way he could maintain a professional relationship with her, in the same office, and still maintain his sanity. Today was proof of that. Not when all he wanted to do, every time he saw her, was kiss her again. And again. Until both their knees buckled.

Rick shook himself. Man did not live on sensory flashbacks alone.

With new resolve, he dug through the pile on his

desk for a trade magazine, and started searching the
ads for available positions.

"Okay," Yvonne said. "Spill it."

Yvonne had dragged her to a cafe around the corner
from the station. Although there wasn't much warmth
in the January sun, Christie had asked Yvonne if she
minded a table out on the patio, where anything she
said could be scattered to the breeze. Christie didn't
know if this was a good idea or not, but the need to
unload was too great.

Yvonne listened to Christie's story with no attempt
to disguise her widening eyes. Her cappuccino cooled
in front of her, barely touched.

When she finished, Christie said, for the second
time, "You know, if you repeat any of this, I have to
kill you."

"Relax. I can keep a secret." Yvonne sipped from
her cooling styrofoam cup. "But it's a lulu."

Christie took a big swig of her own cappuccino, like
a sailor knocking back whiskey. After nearly three
months on the overnight shift, coffee didn't make her
bounce off the walls any more. It was becoming a
permanent part of her system.

Yvonne shook her head. "You and Rick. Between
the two of you, you drink enough caffeine to power a
city. You *must* be meant for each other."

"Not when we both work for KYOR."

"You know, women have fallen for the boss before.
Sometimes they live happily ever after."

"Not when the job is so important."

"This is radio, hon, it's not brain surgery."

"I know. But there's not another station within a hundred miles of here, except in L.A., and I'm not ready for that. I know it's just a starting point, but I love my job. And where else would I go?"

"Didn't anyone ever tell you that in this business, you have to be ready to move?"

"I know. But then I found this, and it seemed so perfect."

Yvonne sat back, folding her arms for warmth. "Well, maybe you could get away with it."

"With what?"

"Dating Rick."

"No. It's against company policy." *And he's not asking.*

"Does the company have to know?"

"How long does something like this ever stay a secret?"

"Good point." Yvonne smirked. "Rob and one of the part-timers were sneaking off to the station van for a while a year or so back, and they were the only ones who thought it was a secret. It was a big joke for a while."

"That's what I mean. Who'd ever take me seriously again?"

"Seriously." Yvonne repeated the word thoughtfully. "Maybe that's your problem. Are you always so dead serious about everything?"

"Pretty much. Remember, I was a loan processor for three years." She shuddered at the thought of going back.

"Maybe you need to rethink your priorities. You

know what happens if the transmitter of that radio station blows up?"

"Big FCC violation?"

"See, that's your problem. What happens is, *life goes on*. People are born, they get married, they die, they have kids." She frowned. "Okay, not in that order. But *that's* the stuff life is made of. Not the station. And you and Rick don't seem to know that."

"Okay. Would you walk away from that station today for a chance to get married and have babies?"

Her eyes gleamed. "Depends on who the babies come from."

"No, seriously." There was that word again. Christie winced. "Would you be happy with someone if the first thing you had to do was give up something you loved?"

Yvonne bit her lip, and they sat in silence. Finally, Christie said, "I'm sorry, but can I ask you one thing?"

"Sure. What?"

"How did you know there's a treadmill in Rick's apartment?"

Yvonne burst out laughing. "Is *that* what got you going?" She shook her head. "Honey, you're the queen of jumping to conclusions. I've never been there. Never seen it. Rick got the thing when he turned thirty. He started complaining about picking up a few extra pounds, or something like that. He talked about that treadmill on the air for weeks. Milked it for all it was worth."

Christie waved it away. "I'm sorry. I just wondered..."

"Rick and me?" Yvonne shook her head. "No. Not

ever. We kid around sometimes, but that's *because* it's
just a joke. Rick's the most professional guy I've ever
worked with. It's kind of like on *Star Trek*. Rick is
Captain Kirk, and the station is his Starship Enter-
prise."

"So what does that make me? Space bimbo of the
week?"

Yvonne laughed. "Oh, Christie. I love you."

"Great," Christie said. "Under company policy, *you*
I can date."

This time they both laughed.

"Thanks for listening, Yvonne. I'm sorry I was such
a—"

"Forget it. You've been dragging this thing around
for weeks."

"So, what if you were in my shoes? What would
you do?"

Yvonne squinted pensively. "Either let the guy drag
me off by my hair . . ."

Christie shook her head. Rick wasn't volunteering
to do that, anyway.

"Then I'd find someone else to fall for, fast. Or I'd
start sending demo tapes to other stations."

That night, Christie loaded a cassette into the air
check machine in the studio. She'd improved a lot in
the last couple of months, and if she was going to find
another job, this demo tape had better be good.

In the days that followed, Christie sent out tapes and
became a master at avoiding Rick around the station.
There was no point in risking any further contact. She

wasn't sure what she was more afraid of: another blowup, or of how she'd react if he were nice to her. Those Christmas kisses—and everything leading up to them—had some long-term repercussions. Too many things carried some reminder of him. Everything from Chinese food to her car, which now started with a roar, thanks to the alternator the garage had replaced at a suspiciously low price.

The nights alone in the studio were the worst. All her life, music had pulled at her emotions. Now it hit her so hard she felt like she was missing a layer of skin. The sad love songs were too close to home, while the happy ones mocked her with images of lovers climbing the skies as high as the highest star. At least "Key Largo" was off the play list, after an inordinately long stay. It had shown up in the rotation of songs shortly after that conversation at Rick's apartment, when she'd told him about her early obsession with Bogie and Bacall. Christie had finally asked Yvonne to take it off.

Then there were the commercials. Rick was on far too many of them for Christie's taste. One minute, he was coaxing her out for an evening of fine dining; a few minutes later, he was promising her the deal of a lifetime on a used car. The fact that he was just as convincing on either one should have told her something, she thought. The eternal chameleon, he could change color as the situation warranted.

At first, Christie sent resumes and tapes to radio stations on the West Coast, but she quickly broadened her search. She was prepared to move to Podunk, Iowa if she had to.

What she wasn't prepared for, on the day of her first live appearance, was to arrive at the station and find Rick already loading the van.

Chapter Ten

"Hey, I'm supposed to be doing that." She approached the van, wary of this latest new wrinkle.

"Just giving you a head start." Rick lifted a crate full of extension cords. "Don't worry, I'll be letting you do all the setup. So the earlier we get there, the better."

Her worst suspicions were confirmed. "You're coming along?"

"Who else?" Rick smiled. Either he had amnesia, or he was a gifted actor. "I don't see any reason to bring another full-timer in on a Sunday afternoon. Remember, program directors have no lives." He lifted a speaker and loaded it in. The other one, she noticed, was already inside. His memory was working, all right.

Like Christie, Rick was wearing a station staff shirt, but his definitely fit him better, the sleeves hugging his upper arms as he loaded in another crate. Christie's shirt had just come in last week, silk-screened with her name and the blue and gold KYOR logo. It had been a minor thrill to put it on for the first time, but the manufacturer definitely had a different idea of "small" than she did. The sleeves hung down to her elbows, and the shirt itself was so long it nearly covered her bottom. She'd done her best to tailor it by tucking it in and cuffing the sleeves.

"You don't have to do this," she said. "Yvonne took me along on her broadcast at the clothing outlet last week. She walked me through the whole thing." In spite of her arguments, Christie knew that having backup on her first live appearance made sense. She also knew that having Rick there would make her a nervous wreck.

"You can't be too safe," he said, still unperturbed. "Believe me. There are a lot of little things that can go wrong. I've seen power go out on the equipment, microphones die. . .and don't tell her I told you, but on Yvonne's first remote, she locked herself out of the van."

"Okay," she said. As if she'd ever had any choice.

Christie got busy helping him load, determined to carry her own weight, literally and figuratively. When all the equipment was inside, she closed the back of the van and took the keys. For the first time, Rick showed what might have been faint discomfort. Apparently, it went against his male instincts to let her drive. Well, too bad.

But he still held the driver's door open for her, and she sighed inwardly. Male instincts indeed.

She'd been worried about what to say during the

ten-minute ride in the van, but Rick took care of that with a running commentary of what to expect when she got there. Christie did her best to concentrate, but it wasn't easy. The front of the van was roomy, but Rick seemed to fill it completely with his long legs, his voice, and his presence.

"You should have a pretty big crowd," he said. "They're having dollar burgers the first hour. And when that dies down, I got hold of a few pairs of movie passes for giveaways."

She glanced at him sideways. "Thanks." Movie passes were always a good draw. Plus, a hamburger restaurant at lunchtime was a natural. And with dollar burgers. . .

She'd look incredibly stupid if she managed to mess it up.

When he ran out of information just before they reached the remote, Rick shifted uncomfortably in the passenger seat. He'd bowed to the situation and let her drive, but it felt wrong. He was the man; he should drive. But she was the disc jockey; it was her remote. He sneaked another sidelong glance at Christie in her new, oversized station shirt. With some tucking, she'd managed to keep it from looking like a tent, but its bulky shape just emphasized how small and slender she was. Rick sighed inwardly. The baggy shirt was further proof that she could distract him no matter what she wore. Just one more reason he would have preferred to drive; it would have forced him to keep his eyes on the road. He looked through the windshield and tried to occupy his mind by thinking of natural disasters. Income tax forms. Boy Scout knots.

As long as this situation went on, that was what he had to do.

". . .Now, mount the speakers in the stands, *carefully* . . ." Rick narrowed his eyes at her as they set up the equipment. It was the first time either of them had referred, directly or indirectly, to the speaker incident.

He seemed to be playing it for laughs. Christie took a chance. "Absolutely," she agreed. "Wouldn't want to hurt the speakers." She threw in a smile to show she was kidding, too.

Christie attached the first speaker to its mount on the metal pole. Rick held the stand steady, but otherwise let her do the work. She made sure it was secure before she let go.

When it held, she asked, "How's the foot?"

"Fine. Just don't step on my toes. Next speaker." There was no inflection in his voice. He handed her the second stand to set up.

She pulled up the collapsible pole of the stand to its full height, about a foot shorter than Christie. It reminded her of a tent pole. "This makes me think of camping," she said.

Rick's eyebrows lifted. "You're not going to tell me you're a woman who actually likes camping."

"I love it. I just went a few times, with my boyfriend in college."

"And this manly man had you setting up the tent?"

"Well, I helped." She giggled at the memory. "Although one of us didn't do a very good job. One night in Yosemite, the tent fell down."

"I see." He studied her. "The tent just sort of *fell*

down." His face was a perfect deadpan, but his eyes glimmered, implying all sorts of tent-shaking shenanigans.

"It did! We weren't—I mean—" She felt herself blush, and knew any further protests would only make it sound worse. "The point is, it was raining, and it was too dark to fix it—"

Rick nodded wordlessly. Instead of smiling, he kept looking at her with that mock seriousness, which was even worse.

"So we spent the night sleeping under flat, wet plastic," she finished awkwardly.

"Mm-hmm. Well, at least it doesn't look like rain." Rick handed her the second speaker and stood close by as she secured it into place. "So, what happened?"

"I told you! Nothing."

He burst out laughing, and Christie steadied the speaker. She'd only *thought* she was embarrassed before.

"I meant, to the boyfriend," Rick said. "Did you bury him out in the woods, or what?"

Oh. Christie waited for her face to cool. It was still a fairly personal question. But there wasn't anything very personal in the answer; like most of her past, it was pretty mundane. "He graduated. Moved to Washington, D.C. Last I heard, I think he was working for some congressman or other."

Actually, he'd asked her to marry him. Christie had been shocked. They'd dated for three years, but he'd been her first serious boyfriend, and at that point in her life, a long-term future had never entered her mind.

Her answer seemed to satisfy Rick. He was busy

checking wires. Apparently he hadn't been that curi-ous after all.

By the time they were done setting up, it was nearly noon. Christie realized she'd had precious little chance to be nervous. In fact, she was beginning to enjoy herself. It was almost time to start, and she felt the now-familiar thrill of panic. Rick made sure she knew how to work the equipment that connected her with the jock back at the studio, so she could broadcast her breaks. Then he stepped back. "It's all yours from here," he said. "I'm just here for backup in case you run into trouble."

His hand brushed her arm, just barely a touch, as he turned away. Christie felt an unexpected shiver of goose bumps and looked back over her shoulder to see if Rick had noticed. But he was walking away, toward the canopied sidewalk of the little strip mall that was home to the new Bonker's Burgers.

At the weekend disc jockey's cue from the studio, Christie spoke brightly into the microphone: "Hi, this is Christie Becker with KYOR, broadcasting live at the grand opening of Bonker's Burgers. And if you're hungry, come on down . . ."

Dollar burgers were quite a draw, thank you very much.

In no time, Christie was besieged by listeners who didn't know her from Adam, but who were very in-terested in one dollar hamburgers and any prizes they could get their hands on. She staved them off with station bumper stickers, but on Rick's advice, held on to the movie passes until the mania subsided. She felt dwarfed by the crowd, so when she was making announcements, she adopted a perch on a three-foot-high block of cement at the base of a light pole. Rick was hanging back as promised, but from the sidewalk of the little strip mall, she thought she caught a grin.

She was standing on the light pole base, about to bait the crowd with the first pair of movie tickets, when the speakers abruptly stopped playing the radio station. Christie glanced around and spotted the trouble: a baby stroller had pulled loose the power cord near the restaurant's entrance. Before she could jump down to correct the problem, Rick was there, plugging the cord back in before the song on the air had finished the chorus. Christie caught his eye and nodded her thanks.

Click.

There it was again, she could have sworn it. From halfway across a busy parking lot. Professional chemistry, she reminded herself, as Rick faded back into the crowd.

The lunch crowd had thinned out, and the remote was in its last hour, when Yvonne pulled up. Christie went over to greet her as she climbed out of her car. "I thought I'd try a burger," Yvonne said.

Christie hugged her with a grin. "You lie like a rug. This remote has more reinforcements than the SWAT team."

"Okay, you win. I wanted to see how you're doing. You sound great."

"Thanks. It was a madhouse for a while, but it's been fun."

Yvonne's eyebrows arched. "Any trouble with Rick?"

"So far, so good."

"I thought I'd see if I could give him a lift back to the station, now that you've had a chance to prove you're not going to burn the place down."

Christie considered. It might be a good idea. Things were going well, but then there was the ride back in the van. And there was that *click*.

Rick's voice came from Christie's right. "That's okay, Yvonne. I'll help her tear down."

It was her first uncomfortable moment in the last two hours. Christie glanced at her watch. "Here comes my break," she said, and escaped to her cement perch.

Yvonne tried once more. "You're sure you don't want a ride back?"

"I'm fine." He smiled at her, and it was indistinguishable from any other smile she'd seen on him in the past three years. "Come on, Yvonne," he said lightly, "what do you think I'm going to do to her?"

His casual grin stayed firmly in place. Did the man have a single nerve in his body? He obviously knew she had some idea what had gone on between him and Christie, but he looked her right in the eye. Yvonne gave up. "How's she doing?"

"Terrific." Rick looked across the parking lot, and Yvonne followed his eyes.

Christie stood on the cement block, holding the movie passes high over her head. The sunlight hit her hair and turned it into red-gold fire. "I've never felt so popular," she told the crowd, shaking the prize drawing box tantalizingly.

Yvonne turned back to Rick. He was still looking at Christie, and in that moment, *all* he was doing was looking at Christie. She should have spotted it from the start, back when the always cool, collected and congenial Rick Fox had practically yelled at her when she questioned him about the girl. The man was smitten. *If anyone ever looked at me that way,* Yvonne thought, *I'd melt in a puddle at his feet.*

"And the winner is. . ." Christie juggled the microphone, passes and prize drawing box with surprising ease. "Sharon Wild!" She brandished the winning prize drawing slip as if she were awarding a Grammy. Amid a light smattering of applause, she hopped down and handed the tickets to a pretty brunette woman.

No one was going to get that worked up over someone else's movie passes, but the crowd obviously liked her. And she was playing it for all she was worth. It was, admittedly, a sight to behold.

Yvonne said, "She's something else, isn't she?"

Rick turned back, and the faraway look was gone, with no evidence that it had ever been there. He was good, all right. But Yvonne knew what she'd seen. "She does a great job," he acknowledged.

Yvonne couldn't keep her mouth shut. "You're going to lose her, Rick." She stopped herself there. He could take it whichever way he wanted, personally or professionally. Because whichever way he wanted, it was true.

Rick examined her. "Do you know something I don't?"

Careful. She hadn't driven over here to put Christie in hot water. "I know someone like her doesn't do overnights forever."

"Is she looking?" Rick's scrutiny deepened. She shouldn't have said anything.

"She hasn't mentioned it." *But I told her she should start looking.*

Rick's tone was neutral. "So what do you suggest?"

Sweep her up and carry her off? It might solve Christie's personal problem, but not her professional problem. "I don't know. Give her a raise?"

Rick laughed. "For the overnight shift? When she's barely been here three months? Management would love that. I've been trying to get more money for you for the last year and a half."

Yvonne frowned. "I only asked for that raise a few months ago."

"Yeah, well. It's not my fault you're slower than me." Rick stepped back. "You'd better get some lunch. Assuming that's why you came."

Christie was on a natural high as they packed up the van after the remote. She thought it had gone well; it made her less worried about the number of items she carried. It was hard to remember how uncomfortable she'd been a few hours before. She and Rick worked smoothly side by side, and he kept her laughing with a steady stream of anecdotes about past radio disasters.

"You've sure got some war stories," she said.

"You get some, after fourteen years."

She'd had a question in the back of her mind for a long time. Now seemed like as good a chance as any to ask. "Rick, why did you leave L.A.? I mean, I know there was a lot going on then, but . . ."

"That's one of my worst stories." He was winding

a long orange extension cord with the expertise of long practice. The winding slowed. "But I guess it's another good lesson in Ugly Radio Truth." He slapped the cord into the plastic crate and picked up the next one. After a long pause, he looked at Christie, but he seemed to be seeing somewhere past her. "When Sylvia left, it made the station grapevine. And there was someone standing by to take advantage of the situation. We had an overnight guy who was as enterprising as you, only he wasn't as nice about it. About that time, we got a new program director, and that didn't help." Another bundle of cord went in with a slap. "One night, an empty bottle of Scotch turned up in the studio. It wasn't mine." His eyes held hers, as if to be sure she believed him, but Christie didn't doubt it. He had no reason to lie to her, or even to tell the story. "So there were accusations, and of course I denied it. You have no idea how hard it is to be convincing when you're denying flat-out lies. I didn't use the word 'framed,' because that sounds so paranoid, but—" He shrugged.

"They fired you?"

"Oh, no. They're not stupid. That's a lawsuit waiting to happen." He smiled ironically. "In fact, all would have been forgiven if I'd come clean and done a stint in rehab. That's the twisted part. If I'd been a falling-down drunk, I might still be there today. No, out of the goodness of their hearts, they took my word for it. It wasn't until a few weeks later that they announced some changes were being made. They were bumping me to overnights, and the overnight guy was getting my shift. They didn't dare fire me, but they could nudge me out the door. It worked."

"That *is* an ugly story."

"It's a little tawdry." He shrugged, then smiled again, looking as though he'd just brushed himself off. "If it eases your mind any, I don't think they come much worse than that." He took the last speaker stand from her and loaded it into the back of the van.

"What happened after that? You couldn't find an opening in Los Angeles?"

"Well, at first I didn't try. I sold furniture for a few months, if you can picture that. When I look back, I think I was actually trying to make myself as miserable as I could." They were done loading, but to Christie's surprise, Rick took a seat on the open back of the van, resting his arms on one raised knee. She considered joining him, but decided it was better not to get that close.

"When I did look," he said, "I got two offers. One was for seven to midnight again, at another L.A. station. The other one was afternoon drive here. They promoted me to program director about a year after that. I made the right choice." He looked at her as if he expected her to argue the point. "The thing is, Los Angeles is a very competitive market. I don't mind competition, but some of the forms it takes—" He shook his head. "You've got people from major cities all over the country climbing over each other to get there. And once you do, you're always looking over your shoulder, wondering if someone else is after your job. Your coworkers aren't friends, they're competitors. All these years later, I'm still in touch with people from Fresno, Antelope Valley, San Bernardino . . . but not one person from Los Angeles. A friendship like you and Yvonne—it wouldn't happen. Instead of being glad for the help, she'd be afraid you were after her job."

Christie's eyes widened. "I never even thought—"

"Of course you didn't. And neither did she. That's what's nice about a market this size. If you can find something that pays enough. I admit that's not easy." He shook his head again. "I'm rambling. I guess all I'm saying is, Christie . . . it's not always a nice place out there. Make sure you know what you want." His eyes were fixed on hers, and Christie had the feeling this was the first honest conversation he'd had with her since Christmas. No longer the affable chameleon, he was speaking directly to her. And she still wasn't sure what he meant.

He was looking at her so seriously. What was he trying to tell her?

Rick stood. "Just something to think about, when you move on." He turned to close the back of the van. She couldn't see his face.

Christie felt a surge of guilt over the tapes she'd sent out. He couldn't know about that. Could he? "Trying to get rid of me?" she asked lightly.

"Of course not." Rick slammed the door shut. "Just another ugly radio truth." He took the keys from the lock and held them up, his professional smile back in place. "Mind if I drive on the way back? Sorry. It's a man thing."

What was the difference between working three hours together on a remote, and driving ten minutes together back to the station? The silences began to grow. She watched Rick with his hands on the wheel, eyes straight ahead.

Two blocks from the station, he broke one of the silences. "By the way, I won the bet."

"What bet?"

"Ninety days today. And it doesn't look like you've snapped."

"Oh." *That was today?* "Hey, wait. I didn't bet against myself."

"Then I guess we both win." He spared her a glance for the briefest of smiles.

Christie found a smile to match it. "So what's my prize?"

"I don't know. Let's see. . ." Rick's eyes went back to the road. "Station T-shirt? Oh, wait, you're already wearing one. Your first remote? No, you just did one. And passed with flying colors, by the way."

Christie's throat ached. That was the boss talking. "Thanks."

"By the way, you left your headphones in the studio again over the weekend. That's a really good way to get them thrashed, or stolen. I put them in the file drawer in my office." His tone was stern and matter-of-fact. "If you're going to leave them at the station, keep them there. I told you that before."

Christie only vaguely remembered the conversation. "Yes, sir."

By the time they pulled up to the station, her natural high had dissipated.

That night, Christie started to get her headphones from the shelf in the studio before she remembered.

Okay, so sue me. It's a habit. Sighing, she got her keys and headed for Rick's office.

When she opened the drawer of the wide, horizontal filing cabinet, a barrage of color hit her in the face. Balloons.

Christie shrieked and laughed at the same time, stepping back as red, green, blue and yellow balloons flew up around her, stopping short of the ceiling. They were tied together and anchored by her headphones. She searched the drawer in vain for a card or note of any kind.

Rob appeared in the doorway, apparently brought by her shriek. He squinted at the balloons, still bobbing around her. "So what is it between you and Rick, anyway?"

"Nothing," Christie said immediately. She felt like a three-year-old caught with stolen cake all over her face. And just as transparent.

"Right," Rob said, still surveying the balloons. "And I'm Cleopatra. If I ever laid a hand on you, I think he'd cream me." The thought of Rick "creaming" anyone on her behalf was laughable. But Christie realized that lately, Rob's flirting had tapered way down.

He poked at a green balloon, then turned and headed back for the studio. "Last song's on."

Christie stared, dumbfounded, at Rick's little multicolored salute. She had to squash her feeling of delight over the gesture. Feelings like that only spelled her death sentence here at the station. She thought about the kiss, the turtle, their long talk today, and the genial mask he'd been wearing all this time. She still wasn't sure who the real Rick Fox was, but she was sure about one thing.

She had to get out of there fast.

Chapter Eleven

Rick got the call before he'd gotten his coffee. It was from a station in Tucson, asking about Christie.

He knew this was going to happen, and he'd already made up his mind what he would say. It would have been easy enough to damn her with faint praise. Just a few carefully chosen qualifiers about how well she was doing. . .for a beginner. It would keep her here longer. Instead, Rick told the truth, his fist clenched around the receiver. He had no right to do anything else.

He hung up and pushed back from his desk. He hadn't been socked in the stomach since he was twelve, but he recognized the way it felt. What he had a harder time remembering, strangely, was how it had felt only five years ago when Sylvia left. He was pretty sure it hadn't been like this.

Rick didn't know how many other applicants the people in Tucson were looking at, but the fact that they'd telephoned the program director at Christie's station was not a good sign. Not for him, anyway.

Time was running out.

Tucson. At least seven or eight hours away. If she got the gig, she'd have to move, and he wouldn't be surprised if he ended up volunteering to help load the truck. All in the name of—what? Friendship?

He rested his head on the back of his chair and shut his eyes. It didn't help much, but it did shut out the sight of his desk, with its ever-changing stacks of clutter. He'd spent many a night there, digging into those stacks, when his apartment seemed too empty to go to. At times it had been a solace, a home away from home, but lately he'd begun to despise it. Three months ago, he and Christie had sat for the first time with that desk between them. In a way, it had stood between them ever since.

Lately, after hours, he'd packaged up a lot of resumes from this spot. Now it looked like Christie might beat him to the punch.

"Rick?" Yvonne's voice came from several feet away.

"Mm-hmm?" He didn't move.

"Are you okay?"

Reluctantly, he opened his eyes. She'd stopped in the doorway, headphones in hand, on her way down the hall to start her air shift. Now she was staring at him with a mixture of concern and curiosity. "What's wrong?"

He smiled weakly. "Nothing. Just that Reyes Curse of yours."

He shouldn't have said it. He wouldn't have, if the shock hadn't been so fresh.

"Christie?"

"Yeah. That." He straightened, pinching the bridge of his nose. Pulling the chair back up to his desk, he started to reach for his coffee mug, and remembered it was sitting next to the machine in the break room, waiting for the next pot to finish brewing. Bad news before coffee. Not fair.

"Did she quit?" Yvonne's voice was hushed.

"No." *Not yet.* He shook his head. "Forget it. I shouldn't have said anything."

"Sure you don't want to talk about it?"

"Men don't talk. Men have ulcers. It's why you outlive us."

She wasn't taking the hint. She still stood there, watching him. He didn't know how much she knew, but he knew it was way too much. Men didn't talk, but women did. "Rick, you're not going to let her go without a fight, are you?"

He raised his eyebrows at her. "Don't you have an air shift to do?"

Yvonne arched her eyebrows in return, then left without another word.

Rick sighed, pulled himself up and trudged to the coffee machine.

Christie plugged in her headphones with a heavy heart. These night shifts were getting longer and longer, and more and more sad ballads seemed to be cropping up on the play list. She knew it was her imagination, but it didn't help.

It was Thursday night—no, Friday morning, she corrected herself—and she had an interview in Tucson first thing Monday. Rick had asked very few questions when she'd asked to take the Monday shift off. Instead, he'd waved her away, saying she had that much comp time coming to her for all the extra work she put in. For a moment she'd stood there in front of his desk, tempted to say more, but he seemed more preoccupied than usual. Probably just as well.

She had an interview to work the midday shift in Tucson, for a lot more money, and she was miserable.

Christie started the next song. Paul McCartney's voice filled the studio, singing warmly and sweetly about no more lonely nights. It was one of her favorites, but it wasn't on the play list. She'd cued the wrong track on the CD player. And tonight, it was the last thing she needed to hear. A lot of the songs that were getting to her these days were pretty sappy. But this one, with its mixture of longing and hope, felt intimate and real. Christie reached for the knob to change to the right track, then stopped. Perversely, she bit her lip and let it play.

"No more lonely nights. . ." Paul sang.

It was too much. She dropped her forehead to her arms on the counter and waited for the phone to ring, for Rick to tell her the thing wasn't on the stupid play list. Half of her hoped he would.

But he didn't.

The first hour of the night dragged by. Then the song on CD-1 started to skip, and Christie reached for the butter knife before she realized this wasn't the problem CD player. The glass walls around her started to vibrate. Then, invisible hands seemed to be shaking the whole studio from the outside as the tremor grew.

An old hand at California earthquakes, Christie ducked underneath the counter. She knew a lot of people who didn't even bother to do that. There wasn't much room, but she managed to find some cover alongside the sound equipment and dusty wires. Around her, the room continued to rock, and she eyed the rattling windows with some apprehension. At least there were blinds in front of the glass.

Most earthquakes were over in a few seconds. This one was still picking up steam. Christie was willing to bet most people would be diving for cover by this time. CDs fell—no, flew—from the shelf above her, sailing by and clattering to the floor.

Finally, slowly, it subsided.

Christie straightened, not sure if what she felt was some remaining swaying or her own reaction to the movement. The quake must have gone on for the better part of a minute. Now, it was barely over, and already her phones were lighting up. It was a foreign sight this time of night.

Priorities, she reminded herself. Christie went on the air, confirmed that there had been an earthquake, and details would be available soon. She checked the Internet, found the initial assessment of the quake, and started answering phone calls. It had been a big one, originating about twenty miles away...

Then the EAS tone sounded, and all bets were off.

The Emergency Alert System was tested on a regular basis, but Christie had never heard of it being needed for an actual emergency. She scrambled for the station's EAS manual, which miraculously hadn't fallen off the shelf with the CDs. Following the instructions, she received a message from the emergency crew: a natural gas line had broken in a suburban neighborhood, and the surrounding blocks were being evacuated.

Christie aired the report. The phones were going insane. Answer the phones? Keep the music going? She wasn't sure. Wildly, she remembered what she'd once said to Rick: *So I'm here in case of an emergency?*

Rick. It was after one in the morning, but she had a feeling he'd better know about this. She was picking up the phone, trying to get a line clear to call him, when he hurried into the studio, pulling off his jacket and joining her behind the counter. Obviously the quake had gotten him out of bed; his hair was rumpled, and so was his shirt, as if he'd thrown it on in a hurry. He looked more unshaven than she'd ever seen him. And Christie had never been so glad to see anyone in her life.

"I missed the last couple of minutes," he said. "What have we got?"

"EAS alert. I just aired a report from the emergency crew. There's a gas main. . ."

And suddenly the chaos was manageable. It was a frenzy, but with Rick's help, it was a controlled frenzy. He handled the phone calls and helped her run the control board; Christie took the updates from the emergency crew and aired the reports. Even at this hour, the evacuation had created a traffic backup in the mountain pass leading out of the neighborhood near the gas line. Most of the calls were superfluous, asking about the reason for the backup, or what the magnitude of the earthquake had been. All of which the callers would have known if they'd turned on their radios for five minutes. Rick waded through them and passed the few valid tidbits of information on to Christie.

It made the afternoon drive shift look like a cake walk, but they were getting through it.

After the first hour, the panic began to level off. Evacuees were leaving their homes; people routed out of their beds by the earthquake were going back to sleep. After one more update, this one from the California Highway Patrol, Christie was able to actually talk to Rick for the first time. "How many EAS alerts have you had?"

"First one. But then, I never had an evacuation before either."

"How'd you get here so fast?"

"Fast? It took me fifteen minutes." It had felt more like five. "I didn't know how bad it was until I got here. But after that quake, I knew the phones alone would have you buried."

"Thanks for coming," she said. He couldn't have slept more than a few hours. But his eyes were alert, and she knew he was riding the same adrenaline rush she was. "The phones, I could have handled. But all this—"

Just when she was starting to catch her breath, another tremor hummed through the studio. Aftershocks could be stronger than the original earthquake, but this time Christie refrained from diving to the floor. Instead, she held on to the sides of the counter with both hands. Rick put one hand on her shoulder, as if to steady her. For the first time it occurred to her just what a small space they were in together—about four feet wide, enclosed by the counter on three sides. Even without his hand on her shoulder, he was close enough for her to feel some of the warmth from his body.

The aftershock passed in a few seconds, barely a rumble.

"Small potatoes," Christie said, nervously taking a step back. Rick let her go, and she cringed as the phones lit up anew.

The crisis ended not with a bang, but with a whimper. The evacuation was completed; word went out that the gas main would be repaired during the day. No fatalities, no injuries reported. Roadblocks were diverting traffic away from the area. The morning commute was going to be a zoo, but that was hours away. At last, the calls tapered off again.

Christie's adrenaline rush ebbed away, as if someone had pulled a drain plug inside her. Two hours working side-by-side with Rick. They'd functioned smoothly as a team, as if that was the way it was meant to be. She couldn't have done it without him. And now it was ending.

She studied Rick as he handled a stray phone call— his tousled brown hair, the studied concentration in his eyes, just a slight weariness creeping in around their corners. It was a face she'd grown all too fond of, and if things worked out right, soon she wouldn't be seeing it any more. He'd been here for her at a moment's notice. But then, that was his job.

Rick hung up. Christie turned away and went on the air with the news that the immediate emergency was over. "We'll have information as it becomes available. Right now, back to more of your favorite music, here on KYOR." She fired off a song, signaling the return of normalcy.

She closed the microphone, and Rick took one more phone call. Like a well-oiled machine, she thought. For another minute or two.

He hung up and turned to her, grinning. "Think we should air a report on a fallen lamp?"

Their eyes met, and Rick's smile faded as they stood there, barely more than a foot apart. Suddenly, a natural disaster was nothing. Being alone in this tiny studio with Rick, at this hour—that was cataclysmic. In spite of the music, a prevailing feeling of quiet settled over the studio. The phone lines stayed dark.

Rick tried another smile, but this one seemed forced. "You've really had a baptism by fire, haven't you?" he said. His conversational tone was jarring. "Barely out of your probationary period, an EAS alert. . ."

The boss makes a pass at you and acts like it never happened. . .

Christie turned away and grabbed for the EAS binder. The alert had to be logged. As she searched for the right place to write it in, her hands started to shake. "You can go now." She took a deep breath and tried to make her voice steadier than her hands. "Get some sleep. I really appreciate—"

She felt his hands on her shoulders. It was like pushing a button; at his touch, her eyes blurred. Christie closed them tight. She was starting to shake, and it wasn't from any EAS alert. She set the book down on the counter before she could drop it.

"Hey," he said softly. "It's all right." Gently, he squeezed her shoulders. "You did a great job."

Christie stiffened at his soothing touch, and a thought hit her with violent force: she never again wanted to hear Rick tell her what kind of *job* she'd done. "I don't care." Her voice was choked.

"You don't mean that," he said. "You're exhausted. And you're fed up. I know." Hands still on her shoulders, Rick gently pulled her backward to lean against him.

She shook her head, not trusting her voice, trying not to accept the firm support of his body against hers. Rick's arms came up around her, and she didn't know what to feel—frustration, exhaustion, anger. She tried to feel anything but the warmth that enclosed her. "It's okay," he whispered. "Just let it go."

What did he expect her to do? Cry? Melt into his arms? She knew where that led. She'd spent the last several weeks dealing with the fallout. He turned her to face him, drawing her head toward his chest.

Christie started to pull away. "We can't—"

"Hush. It's three-thirty in the morning." He stroked her hair, and she let him, the gentleness of his fingers smoothing away her resolve. Once again he drew her closer, and this time she settled her cheek against his chest. He held her firmly, as if he would hold her up all night if he had to. She clenched her teeth and closed her eyes tight, holding it in. Trying not to give in completely.

"Breathe," he reminded her. Christie drew in a long, slow breath, then let it out, shuddering. Some of the tension went out of her. She let her body slump, too tired to fight any more, too tired to hide any more. She allowed herself to feel the warmth of his arms, the firmness of his chest. And then she became aware of the sound of his heart, beating much faster than his soothing words would indicate. "I've got you," he said. "It's all right."

Nothing's all right, she wanted to say.

Peripherally, almost like a sixth sense, she became aware that the song was ending. Christie's hand shot out to the control panel beside them to start the next CD. Her hand bumped into Rick's as he reached for the same button. Christie wasn't sure which one of them actually started the song.

As the music started to play, he took her hand, twining his fingers through hers. He studied their hands for a moment, then looked straight into her eyes. Christie's heart hammered at the naked, exposed look in the gray eyes that searched hers. She tried to pull away, but he held her firmly. "Rick, I have to—"

"Don't say it," Rick pulled her against him, and this time she didn't pull back.

He kissed her. She didn't respond, not at first, but that didn't stop Rick. His lips were insistent and persuasive. The night of the Christmas party might have been an impulse, a fluke, but this was no impulse. This was—something else. A gentle onslaught. Christie tried to hold rigid against it, but she was losing the battle. The pressure of his lips sent a warmth through her that made her weak.

Her resistance faded, then melted. As she dissolved against him and returned the kiss, she felt something loosen inside her. Weeks of holding back seemed to fall away, bit by bit, leaving her emotions stripped bare. She put her arms around his waist, just for something to hold on to, and the space between them closed once again. That other embrace had been tender, melting. This one had a growing urgency, almost a desperation. And again, in the back of her mind, she knew there was going to be a heavy price to pay. Christie brought her arms up, clinging to the taut muscles over his shoulder blades.

Rick felt the pressure of her fingers against his back and wrapped his arms still more securely around her. He heard the sound he remembered so well—that low, tiny moan that seemed to come from somewhere far back inside her. It filled his ears, and it echoed somewhere inside him. She fit so perfectly in his arms, soft, firm and delicate all at the same time. He barely broke the kiss before he started on a new one, determined to keep her fastened to him. If he didn't let go of her, she couldn't leave. It felt that simple.

There would be no going back after this, and he knew it. But he didn't want to go back. He couldn't. No more happy talk in the hallways, no more pretending to be just pals. This was all or nothing. He was going for broke.

Because, for all he knew, he was kissing her goodbye.

Chapter Twelve

When the kiss was over, Rick pulled her close, and Christie felt his cheek rest on top of her head.

"Christie, I know."

She hardly recognized the husky voice as Rick's. One of his hands tangled lazily through her hair. "I know about the job in Tucson." This time he was the one who let out a shuddering breath. "And I don't want you to go."

It was like having two bombs drop in her lap at once.

He knew. And he was asking her not to leave.

She hadn't known until now how badly she'd wanted to hear that. And it didn't do her a bit of good. If she stayed, what then? Quit her job? For a moment, standing with the support of Rick's solid warmth, she found herself considering it. But it should be a happy choice, one she could make with a full heart, and she didn't know if she could do that.

A strange, heavy silence filled the room. It took Christie a moment to figure out why. The last song had run out. And Rick Fox, the man who loathed dead air, didn't move.

After a second or two, Christie couldn't stand it any more. She wrenched away and hit the console to start the next CD player. It was in CD-2, back from the shop once again, and she was paid back for her efforts by the familiar thrumming noise as the song stuck. Christie clenched her teeth, advanced CD-1 to another track, and fired it off instead. She scrambled to load the next song, trying to get things back in order. If she could just deal with things here in the studio—things she had control over—she'd be all right. But her heart was racing.

Rick laughed raggedly. "So who doesn't care any more?"

She didn't want to turn around. It meant facing Rick, and that meant facing the turmoil she was in. So she didn't turn around. She tried to keep her voice steady, even though she was still shaken from the intensity of his kiss. "Rick, I need you to go."

"That's it?" His voice was closer now. She was cornered in the tiny counter area, with Rick behind her and the bank of CD players in front of her. "Just go?"

Christie crossed her arms tight in front of her, clenched her fists and dug her nails into her palms, trying for some external pain to battle what was going on inside her. She felt as if she were filled with broken glass. Everything hurt.

"Come on, Rick, what do you expect?" She forced herself to turn and face him. He was closer than she expected, but she still managed to avoid his eyes. She fixed her gaze instead on the rumpled shoulder of his shirt, where her head had rested a few minutes ago.

He seemed to have recovered from their embrace; his tone was insanely reasonable. "Look, I know it hasn't been easy—"

"Hasn't been easy?" She'd never heard more outrageous words. "It's been easy enough for you."

"That's not true." She made the mistake of meeting his eyes, and her heart thudded faster. They looked so earnest, so sincere. She reminded herself how sincere he could sound when he was advertising yet another never-to-be-repeated offer on the car of her choice. The voice was good, but those eyes could sell a whole fleet of cars. Christie made herself look away again, watching Rick's arm instead as he passed his hand through his hair. "Christie, if you could just wait a little while longer before—"

She shut out the calming voice before he could sell her another bill of goods. "Wait for what? Why *wouldn't* I leave? I can't keep doing this." She'd wanted to keep the emotion out of her voice, but now she couldn't even keep up with the words. They rushed out ahead of her, while she just watched and listened. It was like an out-of-body experience. "What am I supposed to do? Risk my job so we go into another hot clinch for five minutes every month? Or sneak off to the transmitter room for—"

"I never said anything like that."

"You never *say* anything." She looked at him again and tried, as hard as she could, to feel nothing but the anger and frustration she'd been cycling through for the past several weeks. "You just click on and off like a light switch, whenever it suits you."

"Christie, stop." He took her by the shoulders. She backed up against the counter, ramrod straight. He closed his eyes briefly, and Christie watched him draw in a long breath. "There might be another way."

"I know." Her eyes burned. She spoke around the huge ache in her throat. "I know what your *other* way is. One of us quits. Let's see—who would that be? The one who's been at it all these years? Or the one who just started a few months ago?" He started to speak, but she cut him off. If she didn't, she knew she'd cave in. She flailed for something to fight him off. "Even if I did, how do I know you'd even be around a month later? You've chucked one relationship for radio already."

It was a direct hit. Rick's hands dropped away from her shoulders. His face changed. He'd never looked at her so coldly, not even that first day he'd interviewed her. That look had been preoccupied and slightly annoyed. This look was ice. She felt that chill all the way through her—the pit of her stomach, the tips of her toes, but most of all, her heart. And she knew she'd destroyed everything.

He turned and walked out before she could say anything more.

She didn't move again until she heard the outside door close behind him. Christie looked at the clock. It was a quarter to four. Against Rick's long-standing order, she cracked open the blinds. It was dark outside, so she barely caught a glimpse of his rapidly retreating figure walking toward the parking garage. She'd fought him off, all right.

From the speakers behind her, the singer whined out yet another lovesick ballad.

Back at his apartment, Rick dropped onto the couch, his arm over his eyes. So much for going for broke. He'd stuck his neck out, been about to stick it out the rest of the way, when she'd ripped his head off.

Masochistically, he'd listened to her on the short drive home, as Christie recapped the earthquake and the evacuation with smooth competence. There was nothing in her voice to suggest what she'd just been through, unless it was a certain fierce effort to sound just as professional as ever. He recognized that trick from the days after his marriage broke up. The more miserable he got on the inside, the more defiantly cheerful he got on the outside. At least while he was on the air.

You're turning into me, girl, he thought. *And it's not a good idea.*

Rick reached for the phone on the end table by the couch and called the station. He recorded a message at the front desk, explaining the overnight emergency, and said he'd be in later. He'd never called in sick in the five years he'd been there, and he couldn't remember ever calling in late. But he'd better get some rest, even though sleep sounded impossible.

Rick shut his eyes and tried to shut out his thoughts. Christie's last words to him—that final, verbal slap— still burned there. He could try to tell himself she'd just been trying to put the brakes on a hopeless situation. Because she knew it was hopeless, knew it better than he did. But he knew the price of putting a job before a relationship. Knew it better than she did. Maybe, like him, she'd learn the hard way.

Whatever made her say it, one fact was inescapable. It was more true than she knew.

Sylvia's affair had made him angry—furious—and it had hurt. But underneath, there was the sneaking suspicion that it didn't hurt quite the way it should. It was what had made it easier, if not to forgive Sylvia, at least to get back on civil ground. He knew he'd failed at the marriage, too. Not as visibly or dramatically as Sylvia, and maybe not as badly. But he'd been single-minded and more than a little self-centered. His passion for the job, and that ambition to take L.A. by storm, had been all-consuming. He hadn't gone to someone else, but then, he hadn't needed to. If he was honest, he had to admit that his heart was somewhere else to begin with.

But no. He'd been wronged, and he'd practically worn it like a badge, because it put everyone on his side. He could magnanimously say he'd made mistakes too, and still look like a hero by comparison. And when it came to getting close in relationships, it was a comfortable cop-out. *Sorry, can't do that, I've been hurt.*

It was easy. Or it had been, until Christie.

That was all moot now. Because she had an interview in Tucson on Monday, and he had no way to stop her even if he wanted to.

* * *

Definitely not the pink one, Christie thought.

She stared into her closet at the dress she'd worn for her first interview with Rick. That appointment had been a near disaster, and the dress held too many associations for her now anyway. She knew she'd never wear it again. The navy one she'd worn for her second interview wasn't looking like a good choice, either.

Get a grip, she told herself.

It was really too soon to pack for Tucson, at any rate. She wasn't leaving until the day after tomorrow. Her plan was to drive out there Sunday, sleep there that night, and go in fresh for her morning appointment. Afterward, she could make the eight-hour drive back to Santa Moreno and still have time to get several hours of sleep before her air shift.

If Rick still had her on the schedule.

Whether or not she got the job, whether Rick made the official decision or she did, she had to leave KYOR. After last night, that was crystal clear. She would stay out her two weeks' notice, if that was what Rick wanted; by now, they'd both had plenty of practice politely avoiding each other.

She rested her head against the open closet door and refused to cry. She'd managed a few fitful hours of sleep when she got home, only to wake up and remember everything that had gone so wrong last night. Diving under the counter was probably the last smart thing she'd done. Too bad she couldn't have stayed down there. If she had those few hours in the studio to live over again, what would she do differently?

If she had the past few months to live over again, what would she do differently?

Not to have known Rick? Impossible. Not to have been his friend? It was hard to picture. Never to have kissed him? She closed her eyes hard. It hurt, but she wasn't going to cry. It was Friday, so she didn't work tonight, since Friday night was actually Saturday morning. The time between now and the Tucson interview weighed on her. She didn't know what to do with herself. But the one thing she was determined *not* to do was cry over a nonexistent relationship.

She finally decided what she should be doing: writing her letter of resignation.

Chapter Thirteen

Yvonne picked up the phone in the studio. "KYOR."

"Yvonne, it's Christie. Do you need me this afternoon?"

There was something wrong with Christie's voice. Yvonne turned down the monitor speakers, to the point where she could keep track of the music without being distracted by it. "Nothing crucial." Fridays were always a madhouse at the station, but she'd manage. The strain in her friend's voice took priority. "What's wrong?"

"Rick and I were up half the night for an emergency, and—things got bad."

Yvonne had been wondering about that ever since she heard Rick would be late. "The earthquake? I know. Rick called in too. I thought it was a sign of the apocalypse."

"Rick called in?"

"Uh-huh. He told Karen at the front desk he'd be in later. What happened, sweetie?"

"Oh, Yvonne, everything blew last night. He hates me."

"No way," Yvonne said. "I never thought Rick would ever call in. Not unless he got laryngitis so bad he had to tap out a signal in Morse code. That's not hate, honey. That's love."

"You weren't there last night." Christie's tone was flat, dead.

It was time to back-announce the last song. Yvonne cued the next one, instead of interrupting their conversation. "Are you okay, sweetie?"

"Not very. But I will be."

Stubborn. "Well, listen, take it easy. And call me later on. We'll do something tonight, okay? Maybe rent a chick flick."

"That sounds nice." But Christie's voice was still faint. "I'll be down at the station for a few minutes later on this afternoon. I've got something to take care of first."

Christie went back over her resignation letter one more time. Her official reason for leaving—"to pursue other opportunities"—took up the least time and space. She spent the rest of the letter acknowledging both Rick and Yvonne for their encouragement and support. She even included a friendly word about Rob. She didn't know if anyone ever read these things, once they were dropped into a file, but she wanted to put it on record somewhere. She'd done several drafts, until she'd said everything she could think of to say. Still, she wasn't satisfied, and finally Christie admitted to herself why.

What she wanted to say most, she couldn't.

She loved Rick. Loved him as much as she'd ever loved the job, and now she couldn't have either one. She'd made sure of that last night. That cold look when he left told her she'd burned her bridges, but good. And it was just as well. She couldn't stay. It had only been a matter of time before it all fell apart.

Now she could go somewhere else and pursue her dream with a clear head. And if a handsome boss ever looked at her sideways, she'd never look back. She'd keep her eyes straight ahead, on the controls where they belonged, and ignore any possible temptation. But Christie knew there was no danger of that.

She'd never again, in her life, meet another Rick Fox.

Finally, she cried.

A little after one o'clock, Yvonne peered down the hall and saw Rick heading for his office with a bundle of mail tucked under his arm, one letter already open in his hand. He went inside and, for the second time she could remember, closed the door behind him. The plot thickened.

A minute later, her phone lit. The extension number showed that the call was from inside the building. She picked it up. "Studio."

Rick said, "Yvonne, have you heard from Christie?"

"She called a little while ago." Yvonne stood up and leaned over the console, craning her neck to see

Rick's door. It was still closed. "I think she might be coming in later."

"Thanks."

"Rick?" Yvonne couldn't resist. "Where are you calling from?"

"Very funny. If she comes in, let me know, all right?"

"All right." The connection clicked off. Yvonne thought about going across the hall and knocking on the door, but thought better of it. She'd probably done more harm than good already. This time, she was staying out of the middle.

Nearly two hours after his conversation with Yvonne, Rick waited, his door open again. He was on the air in less than an hour. Maybe Christie wasn't coming. Maybe she really was going to leave things the way they were last night. Maybe he should have driven to her apartment instead of coming here, without worrying about whether or not she was ready to see him.

Maybe she was already on her way to Tucson.

His hand was on the phone to call her when she appeared at the door. Rick immediately rose to his feet. And made himself stay put. He couldn't afford to make any more mistakes.

She looked so small, framed in the doorway. Even across the room, her eyes were a little too bright, as though she'd been crying. She walked in with the same stiff posture he'd seen the day he sent her out of the station.

"Christie." He started to move from behind his desk. Stopped. "Close the door, please."

"No, I won't be here for long." She approached the front of his desk purposefully and stood there, ignoring the chair behind her. "Two things." She closed her eyes for a moment, as if to compose herself. When she opened them again, he saw brilliant shades of green and blue, filled with a storm of emotion that threatened to knock him over. There were times when he'd felt he could read Christie well, but today, he didn't dare guess. "Rick, I said something horrible last night, and it wasn't fair. I'm sorry."

His grip on the edge of his desk relaxed. It was enough. More than enough. Her shaky voice alone would have made him forgive her, if he hadn't already. "It's okay. The bleeding stopped around lunchtime." He smiled, but she'd already looked away. He started once again to move around the desk toward her, but this time his legs were frozen. He watched her draw in another deep breath, and knew there was more coming. He had to stop her. "Christie, that's all you need to say. I—"

"No, there's more." She held out a sheet of paper, neatly folded in thirds. "Rick, I can't work for you any more. I quit." She offered the letter to him like a marshal serving a summons, but her voice wavered again.

Her resignation was a given, and it didn't matter now. But insistently, she held out the letter. Rick took it without looking at it, without taking his eyes off her. A few minutes ago, his mind had been swimming with words to say to her. He talked for a living. Why couldn't he say anything now?

"I'm sorry it got so—" Christie brushed back a strand of hair, still looking somewhere past him. He couldn't even move, let alone speak. "I can stay until you find someone, or I can leave right away. Just let me know what you decide." She drew in a shaky breath. "What I can't say in the letter—"

"That's three things."

Finally, he'd found the words to cut her off. Christie stared at him blankly.

"You said you had two things," he reminded her. "You've had your say. Now will you please sit down and let me have my turn?"

So he was still angry. Christie didn't want another confrontation. She backed up a step, and bumped into the chair facing Rick's desk. "I have to go."

"I said, sit down. I love you."

Suddenly, sitting was no problem. She'd been trying to avoid his eyes, but now his gaze had her caught, and it took her breath away. Any trace of this morning's coldness was gone. She couldn't seem to find the glib announcer, or the casual Rick from the hallways either. This was the steady, warm gaze of the man who'd kissed her until she nearly fell over. That look, as much as the words he said, knocked her knees out from under her. Christie landed in the chair. Nothing had really changed, she reminded herself. They were still right where they'd started, with him on one side of the desk and her on the other. *I love you.* "What does that mean?"

"What does it mean?" Rick rested his knuckles on

top of the desk and leaned toward her. "It means I think you're as wonderful as they come. You're beautiful, you're funny, and I love to talk to you. I can't think straight for the first ten minutes I'm around you, and after that, I can't imagine being without you. It means I want us to be together." He held her pinned with that naked gray stare, and his voice went on. Not the disc jockey's voice. This was the voice she'd heard in the studio, hours ago, just before the explosion that had made the earthquake seem small. "And since you haven't run out of the room yet, I'm hoping you feel the same way." He searched her face for a response.

This was it. This was the never-to-be-repeated, once-in-a-lifetime offer, the one she thought she'd already lost. She'd better make up her mind, fast. *Take it. This is real.* There were other jobs, she told herself, and the pang of leaving this one behind couldn't be anything compared to the heartache she'd been feeling all day. She said slowly, "I never thought I'd give this up—"

"I'm not asking you to do that."

Her fragile, slowly building hope crashed just as it was getting off the ground. Was he telling her to leave after all? Christie stared as Rick pulled open a drawer of his desk. She'd long had the feeling that his desk didn't have drawers. Everything just sloshed on top. But now, from the nearly-jammed drawer, he fished out a letter. "Miss Becker, I'm offering you a job."

He passed her the unfolded sheet of paper, gingerly, as if it were made of glass. She thought she felt the paper rattle in his hand as she took it.

At first Christie stared at it without comprehension.

It was on unfamiliar letterhead, from a radio station in Oregon. She couldn't seem to make sense out of what she was reading. It didn't help that she could still feel Rick's eyes, fixed on her, watching for her reaction. "...received your air check... hire you as our morning team..."

She glanced back at the beginning of the letter. It was addressed to both of them.

Christie looked up at Rick, bewildered. He said, "I sent out over thirty tapes."

"Tapes? Of what?"

"Of us. From that week we were on the air together, when you were filling in on news."

"You taped our breaks? Then?" She frowned. "That was before—" she hesitated lamely "—before the Christmas party."

"I know. I wasn't sure why. I just had a feeling we had something special."

"Something clicked," she murmured.

He nodded.

At last comprehension took hold. "You found us a job together."

He nodded again.

She rose to her feet. "You've been looking for how long?"

"Since the beginning of January."

She didn't know whether to hug him or hit him. "Why didn't you tell me?"

"I tried to last night. Before I was so memorably interrupted." His grin was a little crooked.

"But before that—"

"Before that, I had *nothing*. Even last night, I had

nothing. I just got that letter at my apartment today."
He was leaning far over the desk by this time. "Before
that, I couldn't promise you a thing. No assurance I
could get us a gig. You've got three months in radio.
I've got fourteen years, but still, it was a tough sell.
If it hadn't panned out, I would have just been string-
ing you along. I never wanted to do that. So I didn't
say anything." He reached across the desk to brush his
fingertips over her cheek. "Before you came along, I
was pretty good at hiding things. It's not so easy any
more, and I'm really looking forward to giving it up.
What I'd like to hear now," he said in that unfamiliar
husky voice, "is how you feel."

"How I feel?" The question surprised her. "Well,
let's see." Christie tilted her head back and gazed up
at the ceiling, trying to get hold of her whirling
thoughts. "You kiss me, then you treat me like everything's business as usual. You make me a wreck with
mixed signals. You attack me with a drawer full of
balloons. And then you go and find us a job behind
my back." She met his eyes again, surprised to see the
uncertainty there. "Are you serious? I love you."

Rick reached over and took her hand. The pressure
of his fingers was warm and firm around hers. "So is
it a deal? You know what it's going to be like. More
ridiculous hours. More coffee. Probably even more
Top Ramen."

"Mr. Fox," she said, "are you trying to talk me out
of this job?"

"Oh, I gave up on that a long time ago." He smiled,
and Christie couldn't believe she'd ever imagined going anywhere without him. "But we've still got one

thing left to discuss. Our names. Is it Fox and Becker? Or Fox and Fox?" His tone was light, but his eyes were fixed on hers.

"Fox and Fox?"

Rick nodded. "Personally, I think we'd play better as a husband and wife team."

A smile spread over her face. "Is that a job requirement?"

"No," he said, "but if you want to, I could make it one."

"All right," she said. "Anything to help the ratings."

"Well, since I need to clear my desk anyway—" In one sweeping gesture, Rick leaned down and shoved the mounds of paper from the top of his desk, sending them to land in a heap on the floor. Then he reached for Christie and pulled her across the desktop, meeting her in the middle.

"What's this?" she asked as his arms folded around her. "Right here in front of God and everybody?"

"I told you to close the door," he said.

And their lips met, in a kiss they didn't have to hide from anyone.

23705431R00104

Made in the USA
Charleston, SC
30 October 2013